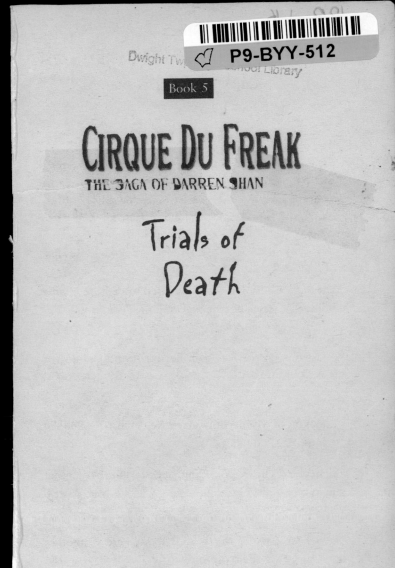

Book 5

CIRQUE DU FREAK

THE SAGA OF DARREN SHAN

Trials of
Death

Book 5

CIRQUE DU FREAK
THE SAGA OF DARREN SHAN

Trials of Death

by Darren Shan

 LITTLE, BROWN AND COMPANY
New York · Boston

Little, Brown and Company

Hachette Book Group USA
1271 Avenue of the Americas, New York, NY 10020
Visit our Web site at www.lb-teens.com

First U.S. Mass Market Edition 2005

First published in Great Britain by Collins in 2001

Library of Congress Cataloging-in-Publication Data

Shan, Darren.
    Trials of Death / by Darren Shan. — 1st U.S. ed.
        p.   cm. — (The saga of Darren Shan ; bk. 5)
    Sequel to: Vampire Mountain.
    Summary: Darren begins the Trials of Initiation to prove himself
worthy of being a half-vampire, even as the clan's blood foes, the
vampaneze, gather near Vampire Mountian.
    ISBN 0-316-00095-7 (mm)
    [1. Vampires. 2. Contests — Fiction. 3. Horror stories.]
I. Title: At head of title: Cirque Du Freak. II. Title.
    PZ7.S52823   Tr 2003
    [Fic] — dc21

MM: 10   9   8   7   6   5   4   3   2

Q-BF

Printed in the United States of America

For:

Nora & Davey — ever-gracious hosts

OBEs (Order of the Bloody Entrails) to:
The enormous, fearsome Emily Ford
Kellee "take no prisoners" Nunley

Mechanics of the Macabre:
Biddy & Liam
Gilly & Zoë
Emma & Chris

PROLOGUE

IF PEOPLE ever tell you vampires aren't real — don't believe them! The world's full of vampires. Not evil, shape-changing, cross-fearing creatures like in the legends, but honorable, long-living, extrastrong beings who need to drink blood to survive. They interfere as little as possible in the affairs of humans and never kill those they drink from.

Hidden away in some snowy, barely accessible corner of the world stands Vampire Mountain, where vampires meet every twelve years. The Council (as they call it) is controlled by the Vampire Princes — who are obeyed by all vampires — and most of those in attendance are Vampire Generals, whose job is to govern the walking undead.

In order to present me to the Princes, Mr. Crepsley had dragged me along to Vampire Mountain and the

Council. Mr. Crepsley's a vampire. I'm his assistant, a half-vampire — my name's Darren Shan.

It was a long, hard journey. We traveled with a friend of ours, Gavner Purl, four wolves, and two Little People, strange creatures who work for a mysterious master by the name of Mr. Tiny. One of the Little People was killed on the way by a mad bear that had drunk the blood of a dead vampaneze (they're like vampires, except they have purple skin and red eyes, nails, and hair — and they *always* kill when they feed). The other then spoke — the first time ever that a Little Person had communicated with anyone — and told us his name was Harkat Mulds. He also delivered a chilling message from Mr. Tiny: a Vampaneze Lord would come into power soon and lead the purple-skinned killers into war against the vampires — and win!

Finally we arrived at Vampire Mountain, where the vampires lived in a network of tunnels and large caves. There I made friends with a bunch of vampires, including Seba Nile, who'd been Mr. Crepsley's teacher when he was younger; Arra Sails, one of the few female vampires; Vanez Blane, a one-eyed games master; and Kurda Smahlt, a General who was going to become a Prince soon.

The Princes and most of the Generals weren't impressed with me. They said I was too young to be a vampire and criticized Mr. Crepsley for blooding me. To prove myself worthy of being a half-vampire, I had to undertake the Trials of Initiation, a series of tough tests usually reserved for budding Generals. When I was making up my mind to accept the challenge, they told me that if I passed, I'd be accepted into the vampire ranks. What they neglected to tell me until afterward (when it was too late to back out) was that if I failed — I'd be *killed!*

CHAPTER ONE

THE HUGE CAVERN known as the Hall of Khledon Lurt was almost deserted. Except for those sitting at my table — Gavner, Kurda, and Harkat — there was only one other vampire present, a guard who sat by himself and sipped from a mug of beer, whistling tunelessly.

About four hours had passed since I learned I was going to be judged in the Trials of Initiation. I still didn't know very much about the Trials, but from the gloomy faces of my companions, and by what had been said in the Hall of Princes, I figured my chances of emerging victorious were, at best, slim.

While Kurda and Gavner muttered on about my Trials, I studied Harkat, who I hadn't seen much of recently (he'd been cooped up in the Hall of Princes, answering questions). He was dressed in his traditional blue robes, although he now wore his hood down, no longer bothering to hide his grey, scarred, stitched-together face. Harkat didn't have a nose, and his ears were sewn underneath the skin of his skull. He had a pair of large, round green eyes, set near the top of his head. His mouth was jagged and full of sharp teeth. Normal air was poisonous to him — ten or twelve hours of it would kill him — so he wore a special mask that kept him alive. He moved it down over his chin when he was talking or eating and back up to cover his mouth when he wasn't. Harkat had once been human but had died and come back in this body, after striking a deal with Mr. Tiny. He couldn't remember who he'd been or what sort of a deal he'd struck.

Harkat had carried a message to the Princes from Mr. Tiny, saying that the night of the Vampaneze Lord was coming. The Vampaneze Lord was a mythical figure whose arrival would supposedly signal the start of a war between the vampires and vampaneze, which — according to Mr. Tiny — the vampaneze would win, wiping out the vampire forces in the process.

Catching my eye, Harkat lowered his mask and said, "Have you . . . seen much of . . . the Halls?"

"A little of them," I replied.

"You must . . . take me . . . on a tour."

"Darren won't have much time for tours," Kurda sighed miserably. "Not with the Trials to prepare for."

"Tell me more about these Trials," I said.

"The Trials are part of our vampiric heritage, going back as long as any vampire can remember," Gavner told me. Gavner Purl was a Vampire General. He was very burly, with short brown hair, and he had a scarred, beaten face. Mr. Crepsley teased him a lot about his heavy breathing and snoring. "In the old nights they were held at every Council," Gavner continued, "and every vampire had to endure them, even if they'd passed a dozen times already.

"About a thousand years ago, the Trials were restructured. This was about the time that the Generals came into being. Before that, there were just Princes and ordinary vampires. Under the new terms, only those who wished to be Generals needed to undertake the Trials. A lot of ordinary vampires take the Trials even if they don't want to be a General — a vampire usually has to pass the Trials of Initiation to earn the respect of his peers — but they aren't required to."

"I don't understand," I said. "I thought if you passed the Trials, you automatically became a General."

"No," Kurda answered ahead of Gavner, running a hand through his blond hair. Kurda Smahlt wasn't as muscular as most vampires — he believed in brains over brawn — and he had less scar tissue than most, although he had three small red permanent scratches on his left cheek, marks of the vampaneze. (Kurda's dream was to reunite the vampires and vampaneze, and he'd spent many decades discussing peace treaties with the murderous outcasts.) "The Trials are only the first test for would-be Generals. There are other tests of strength, endurance, and wisdom, which come later. Passing the Trials just means you're a vampire of good standing."

Good standing was a phrase I'd heard many times. Respect and honor were extremely important to vampires. If you were a vampire of good standing, it meant you were respected by your colleagues.

"What happens in the Trials?" I asked.

"There are many different tests," Gavner said, taking over again from Kurda. "You have to complete five of them. They'll be picked at random, one at a time. The challenges range from fighting wild boars to climbing perilous mountains to crawling through a pit filled with snakes."

"Snakes?" I asked, alarmed. My best friend at the Cirque Du Freak — Evra Von — kept a huge snake, which I'd grown accustomed to but never learned to like. Snakes gave me the creeps.

8

"There won't be any snakes in Darren's Trials," Kurda said. "Our last snake keeper died nine years ago and hasn't been replaced. We still have a few snakes but not enough to fill a tub, never mind a pit."

"The Trials take place one night after another," Gavner said. "A day's rest is all you're allowed in between. So you have to be especially careful at the start — if you get injured early on, you won't have much time to recover."

"Actually, he might get lucky there," Kurda mused. "The Festival of the Undead is almost upon us."

"What's that?" I asked.

"We celebrate with a huge feast when every vampire who's coming to Council has arrived," Kurda explained. "We used the Stone of Blood to search for latecomers a couple of nights ago, and only three more are on their way. When the last arrives, the Festival starts, and no official business may take place for three nights and days."

"That's right," Gavner said. "If the Festival starts during your Trials, you'll have a three-night break. That would be a great bonus."

"If the latecomers arrive in time," Kurda noted gloomily.

Kurda seemed to think I didn't stand a chance in the Trials. "Why are you so sure I'll fail?" I asked.

"It's not that I think poorly of you," Kurda said. "You're just too young and inexperienced. Apart from the fact that you're physically unprepared, you haven't had time to assess the different tasks and practice for them. You're being thrown in at the deep end, and it isn't fair."

"Still whining about fairness?" someone commented behind us — Mr. Crepsley. Seba Nile, the quartermaster of Vampire Mountain, was with him. The pair sat and greeted us with silent nods.

"You were very quick to agree to the Trials, Larten," Kurda said disapprovingly. "Don't you think you should have explained the rules to Darren more thoroughly? He didn't even know that failure to complete the Trials means certain death!"

"Is that true?" Mr. Crepsley asked me.

I nodded. "I thought I could quit if things weren't working out."

"Ah, I should have made it clearer. My apologies."

"A little late for those now." Kurda sniffed.

"All the same," Mr. Crepsley said, "I stand by my decision. It was a delicate situation. I did wrong to blood Darren — there was no hiding from that. It is important for both our sakes that one of us clears our names. If I had the choice, I would face the challenge, but the Princes elected Darren. Their word, as far as I am concerned, is law."

"Besides," Seba Nile added, "all is far from lost. When I heard the news, I hurried to the Hall of Princes and used the old and almost forgotten Period of Preparation clause."

"The what?" Gavner asked.

"Before the time of the Generals," Seba explained, "vampires did not spend years preparing for the Trials. They would draw a Trial at random — as they do now — but rather than tackle it immediately, they had a night and a day to prepare. This was to give them time to practice. Many chose to ignore the Period of Preparation — usually those who had undertaken the Trials before — but there was no dishonor in taking advantage of it."

"I never heard of that rule," Gavner said.

"I did," Kurda noted, "but I'd never have thought of it. Does it still apply? It hasn't been used in more than a thousand years."

"Just because it is unfashionable does not mean it is invalid," Seba chuckled. "The Period of Preparation was never formally abolished. Given that Darren is a special case, I went to the Princes and asked that he be allowed to take advantage of it. Mika objected, of course — that vampire was born to object — but Paris talked him into it."

"So Darren has twenty-four hours to prepare for each Trial," Mr. Crepsley said. "And twenty-four hours to rest afterwards — which adds up to a forty-eight-hour break between each test."

"That is good news," Gavner agreed, brightening up.

"There is more," Mr. Crepsley said. "We also persuaded the Princes to rule out some of the more difficult Trials, those which are clearly beyond Darren's ability."

"I thought you said you weren't going to ask for favors," Gavner noted with a grin.

"And I did not." Mr. Crepsley replied. "I merely asked that the Princes use their common sense. It would be illogical to ask a blind man to paint, or a mute man to sing. So it would be senseless to expect a half-vampire to compete on even terms with a full-vampire. Many of the Trials remain, but those which are clearly impossible for one in Darren's position have been eliminated."

"I still say it's unfair," Kurda complained. He faced the ancient Seba Nile. "Are there any other old laws we could use? Anything about children not being allowed to compete, or that they can't be killed if they fail?"

"None that I am aware of," Seba said. "The only vampires who cannot be killed for failing the Trials of Initiation are the Princes. All others are judged equally."

"Why would Princes be taking the Trials?" I asked.

"Long ago they had to participate in the Trials at every Council, like everybody else," Seba said. "Some still undertake them from time to time, if they feel they need to prove themselves. However, it is forbidden for a vampire to kill a Prince, so if a Prince fails and does not die during the Trial, nobody can execute him."

"What happens in cases like that?" I asked.

"There have not been many," Seba said. "Of the few that I know of, the Princes elected to leave Vampire Mountain and die in the wilds. Only one — Fredor Morsh — resumed his place in the Hall of Princes. That was when the vampaneze broke away, when we needed all of our leaders. Once the crisis had passed, he left to meet his fate."

"Come," Mr. Crepsley said, rising and yawning. "I am tired. It is time to turn in for the day."

"I don't think I'll be able to sleep," I said.

"You must," he grunted. "Rest is vital if you are

going to complete the Trials. You will need to be fully alert, with all your wits about you."

"OK," I sighed, joining him. Harkat stood too. "See you all tomorrow," I said to the other vampires, and they nodded gloomily in reply.

Back in my cell, I made myself as comfortable as possible in my hammock — most vampires slept in coffins, but I couldn't stand them — while Harkat climbed into his. It took a long time to drift off, but finally I did, and though I didn't manage a full day's sleep, I was reasonably clear-headed when night rolled around, and I had to report to the Hall of Princes to learn about my first deathly Trial.

CHAPTER TWO

ARRA SAILS was waiting for Mr. Crepsley and me outside the Hall of Princes. Arra was one of the rare female vampires at Vampire Mountain. She was a fierce fighter, the equal — or better — of most males. We'd fought a contest earlier during my stay, and I'd won her hard-to-earn respect.

"How are you?" she asked, shaking my hand.

"Pretty good," I said.

"Nervous?"

"Yes."

"I was too, when facing my Trials," she said with a smile. "Only a fool goes into them without feeling anxious. The important thing is not to panic."

"I'll try not to."

Arra cleared her throat. "I hope you don't hold what I said in the Hall of Princes against me." Arra had urged the Princes to make me undertake the Trials. "I don't believe in going easy on vampires, even if they're children. Ours is a hard life, not suited to the weak. As I said in the Hall, I think you'll pass the Trials, but if you don't, I won't step in to plead for your life."

"I understand," I said.

"We're still friends?"

"Yes."

"If you need help preparing, call on me," she said. "I have been through the Trials three times, to prove to myself more than anyone else that I am a worthy vampire. There is very little that I don't know about them."

"We will bear that in mind," Mr. Crepsley said, bowing to her.

"Courteous as ever, Larten," Arra noted. "And as handsome too."

I nearly laughed out loud. Mr. Crepsley — *handsome?* I'd seen more appealing creatures in the monkey cages in zoos! But Mr. Crepsley took the compliment in stride, as though he were used to such flattery, and bowed again.

"And you are as beautiful as ever," he said.

"I know." She grinned and left. Mr. Crepsley watched her intently as she walked away, a faraway look on his normally solemn face. When he caught me smirking, he scowled.

"What are you grinning about?" he snapped.

"Nothing," I said innocently, then added slyly, "an old girlfriend?"

"If you must know," he said stiffly, "Arra was once my mate."

I blinked. "You mean she was your *wife?*"

"In a manner of speaking."

I stared, slack-jawed, at the vampire. "You never told me you were married!"

"I am not — anymore — but I used to be."

"What happened — did you get a divorce?"

He shook his head. "Vampires neither marry nor divorce as humans do. We make temporary mating commitments instead."

I frowned. "What?"

"If two vampires wish to mate," he explained, "they agree to share their lives for a set amount of time, usually five or ten years. At the end of that time, they can agree to another five or ten years, or separate. Our relationships are not like those of humans. Since we cannot have children, and live such a long time, very few vampires stay mated for their whole lives."

"That sounds bizarre."

Mr. Crepsley shrugged. "It is the vampire way."

I thought it over. "Do you still have feelings for Arra?" I asked.

"I admire and respect her," he answered.

"That's not what I mean. Do you *love* her?"

"Oh, look," he said quickly, reddening around his throat, "it is time to present ourselves to the Princes. Hurry — we must not be late." And he took off quickly, as though to avoid more personal questions.

Vanez Blane greeted us inside the Hall of Princes. Vanez was a games master, responsible for maintaining the three gaming Halls and watching over the contestants. He only had one eye, and from the left-hand side he looked awful. But if you saw him from the front or right-hand side, you could tell at a glance that he was a kind, friendly vampire.

"How do you feel?" he asked. "Ready for the Trials?"

"Just about," I replied.

He took me aside and spoke quietly. "You can say no if you want, but I've discussed it with the Princes, and they won't object if you ask me to be your Trials tutor. That means I'd tell you about the challenges and help you prepare for them. I'd be like a second in a duel, or a trainer in a boxing match."

"Sounds good to me," I said.

"You don't mind, Larten?" he asked Mr. Crepsley.

"Not at all," Mr. Crepsley said. "I had planned to be Darren's tutor, but you are much better suited to the job. Are you sure it is not an inconvenience?"

"Of course it isn't," Vanez said firmly.

"Then it is agreed." We all shook hands and smiled at one another.

"It feels strange being the center of so much attention," I said. "So many people are going out of their way to help me. Are you like this with all newcomers?"

"Most of the time — yes," Vanez said. "Vampires look out for each other. We have to — everybody else in the world hates or fears us. A vampire can always depend on help from his own." He winked and added, "Even that cowardly scoundrel Kurda Smahlt."

Vanez didn't really think Kurda was a cowardly scoundrel — he just liked to tease the soon-to-be Prince — but many vampires in the mountain did. Kurda didn't like fighting or war and believed in making peace with the vampaneze. To a lot of vampires, that was unthinkable.

A guard called my name, and I stepped forward, past the circular benches to the platform where the thrones of the Princes were. Vanez stood just behind me, while Mr. Crepsley stayed in his seat — only Trials tutors were allowed to accompany contestants to the platform.

Paris Skyle, a white-haired, grey-bearded Prince — he was also the oldest living vampire — asked if I was willing to accept whatever Trial came my way. I said I was. He announced to the hall in general that the Period of Preparation would be used, and that some Trials had been withdrawn, because of my size and youth. He asked if anyone objected. Mika Ver Leth — who'd suggested the Trials — looked unhappy about the allowances and picked irritably at the folds of his black shirt but said nothing. "Very well," Paris declared. "We shall draw the first Trial."

A bag of numbered stones was brought forward by a green-uniformed guard. I'd been told that there were seventeen stones in it, each with its own number. Each number corresponded to a Trial, and the one I picked would be the Trial I'd have to face.

The guard shook the bag and asked if anyone wanted to examine the stones. One of the Generals raised a hand. This was common practice — the stones were always examined — so I didn't worry about it, just focused on the floor and tried to stop the nervous rumblings of my belly.

When the stones had been checked and approved, the guard shook them up once more, then held the bag out to me. Closing my eyes, I reached in, grabbed the first stone I touched, and drew it out. "Number eleven," the guard shouted. "The Aquatic Maze."

The vampires in the Hall mumbled softly among themselves.

"Is that good or bad?" I asked Vanez while the stone was taken up for the Princes to verify.

"It depends," he said. "Can you swim?"

"Yes."

"Then it's as good a first Trial as any. Things could have been worse."

Once the stone had been checked and put aside so that it couldn't be drawn again, Paris told me that I would be expected to report for the Trial at dusk tomorrow. He wished me luck — he said business would keep him away, though one of the other Princes would be present — then dismissed me. Leaving the Hall, I hurried away with Vanez and Mr. Crepsley to prepare for my first test and brush with death.

CHAPTER THREE

THE AQUATIC MAZE was man-made, built with a low ceiling and watertight walls. There were four doors in and out of it, one in each of its four external walls. From the center where I would be left, it usually took five or six minutes to find your way out, if you didn't get lost.

But in the Trial, you had to drag around a heavy rock — half your weight — which slowed you down. With the rock, eight or nine minutes was good going.

In addition to the rock, there was the water to deal with. As soon as the Trial began, the maze started to fill with water, which was pumped in through hoses from underground streams. The water slowed you down even more, and finding your way through the maze usually took about fifteen minutes. If it took longer, you were in serious trouble — because the maze filled to the top in seventeen minutes exactly.

"It's important not to panic," Vanez said. We were down in one of the practice mazes, a smaller version of the Aquatic Maze. The route wasn't the same — the walls of the Aquatic Maze could be moved around, so the maze was different each time — but it served as a good learning experience. "Most who fail in the maze do so because they panic," he went on. "It can be frightening when the water rises and the going gets slower and tougher. You have to fight that fear and concentrate on the route. If you let the water distract you, you'll lose your way — and then you're finished."

We spent the early part of the night walking through the maze, over and over, Vanez teaching me how to make a map inside my head. "Each wall of the maze looks the same," he said, "but they aren't. There are identifying marks — a discolored stone, a jagged piece of floor, a crack. You must note these small differences and build your map from them. That way, if you find yourself in a passage where you've already been, you'll recognize it and can immediately start looking for a new way out, wasting no time."

I spent hours learning how to make mental maps of the maze. It was a lot harder than it sounds. The first few passages were easy to remember — a chipped stone in the top left corner of one, a moss-covered stone in the floor of the next, a bumpy stone in the ceiling of the one after that — but the farther I went, the more I had to remember, and the more confusing it became. I had to find something new in every corridor, because if I used a mark that was similar to one I'd committed to memory already, I'd get the two confused and end up chasing my tail.

"You're not concentrating!" Vanez snapped when I came to a standstill for the seventh or eighth time.

"I'm trying," I grumbled, "but it's hard."

"*Trying* isn't good enough," he barked. "You have to tune out all other thoughts. Forget the Trials and the water and what will happen if you fail. Forget about dinner and breakfast and whatever else is distracting you. Think only about the maze. It must fill your thoughts completely, or you're doomed."

It wasn't easy, but I gave it my best shot, and within an hour I had improved considerably. Vanez was right — cutting off all other trains of thought was the solution. It was boring, wandering through a maze for hours on end, but that boredom was what I had to learn to appreciate. In the Aquatic Maze, excitement could confuse and kill me.

Once my map-making skills were good enough,

Vanez wrapped a long rope around my waist and attached a rock to the other end. "This rock is only a quarter of your weight," he said. "We'll try you with a heavier rock later, but I don't want to tire you out too much ahead of the Trial. We'll get you accustomed to this one first, move up to a rock that's a third your weight, then try you on the real thing for a short time, to give you a taste of how it feels."

The rock wasn't especially heavy — as a half-vampire, I was much stronger than a human — but it was an annoyance. Along with slowing me down, it also had a bad habit of catching on corners or in cracks, which meant I had to stop and free it. "It's important to stop the instant you feel it snagging," Vanez said. "Your natural instinct will be to tug on the rope and free it quickly, but more often than not that worsens the situation, and you wind up taking even longer to fix it. Seconds are vital in the maze. It's better to act methodically and lose four or five seconds freeing yourself than to act hastily and lose ten or twenty."

There were ways to stop the rock and rope from snagging so much. When I came to corners or bends, I had to seize the rope and pull the rock in close to me — that way it was less likely to get stuck. And it was helpful to give the rope a shake every few seconds — that kept it loose. "But you have to do these things automatically," Vanez said. "You must do them without pausing to think. Your brain should be fully occupied with mapping the maze. Everything else must be done by instinct."

"It's useless," I groaned, sinking to the floor. "It'd take months to get ready for this. I don't have a hope in hell."

"Of course you do!" Vanez roared. Squatting beside me, he poked me in the ribs. "Feel that?" he asked, jabbing a sharp finger into the soft flesh of my belly.

"Ow!" I slapped his hand away. "Quit it!"

"It's sharp?" he asked, jabbing me again. "It hurts?"

"Yes!"

He grunted, jabbed me one more time, then stood. "Imagine how much sharper the stakes in the Hall of Death are," he said.

Sighing miserably, I hauled myself to my feet and wiped sweat from my brow. Picking up the rope, I gave it a shake, then started back through the maze, dragging the rock and mapping out the walls, as Vanez had taught me.

———

Finally we stopped for a meal and met up with Mr. Crepsley and Harkat in the Hall of Khledon Lurt. I wasn't hungry — I felt too nervous to eat, but Vanez insisted: he said I'd need every last bit of energy when it came to the Trial.

"How is he doing?" Mr. Crepsley asked. He'd wanted to watch me train, but Vanez had told him he'd be in the way.

"Remarkably well," Vanez said, chewing on the bones of a skewered rat. "To be honest, though I put on a brave face when the Trial was picked, I thought he'd be — excuse the pun — out of his depth. The Aquatic Maze isn't one of the more brutal Trials, but it's one you need a lot of time to prepare for. But he's a quick learner. We still have a lot to fit in — we haven't tried him in water yet — but I'm a lot more hopeful now than I was a few hours ago."

Harkat had brought Madam Octa — Mr. Crepsley's spider — to the Hall with him and was feeding her bread crumbs soaked in bat broth. He'd agreed to take care of her while I was concentrating on my Trials. Moving away from the vampires, I struck up a conversation with the Little Person. "Managing her OK?" I asked.

"Yes. She is . . . easy to . . . take care of."

"Just don't let her out of her cage," I warned. "She looks cute, but her bite is lethal."

"I know. I have . . . often watched . . . you and her . . . when you . . . were onstage . . . at the Cirque . . . Du Freak."

Harkat's speech was improving — he slurred his words a lot less now — but he still had to take long pauses for breath in the middle of sentences.

"Do you think . . . you will . . . be ready . . . for the Trial?" he asked.

I shrugged. "Right now, the Trial's the last thing on my mind — I'm not even sure I'm going to get through the training! Vanez is working me hard. I suppose he has to, but I feel exhausted. I could slide under the table and sleep for a week."

"I have been . . . listening to . . . vampires talk," Harkat said. "Many are . . . betting on you."

"Oh?" I sat up, taking an interest. "What odds are they giving me?"

"They do not . . . have actual . . . odds. They bet . . . clothes and . . . pieces of . . . jewelry. Most vampires . . . are betting . . . *against* you. Kurda and Gavner . . . and Arra . . . are accepting . . . most of the . . . bets. They . . . believe in you."

"That's good to hear." I smiled. "What about Mr. Crepsley?"

Harkat shook his head. "He said . . . he does not . . . bet. Especially not . . . on children."

"That's the sort of thing the dry old buzzard would say," I huffed, trying not to sound disappointed.

"But I . . . heard him talking . . . to Seba Nile," Harkat added. "He said . . . that if you . . . failed, he would . . . eat his cape."

I laughed, delighted.

"What are you two talking about?" Mr. Crepsley asked.

"Nothing," I said, grinning up at him.

When we'd finished eating, Vanez and I headed back to the maze, where we practiced with heavier rocks and in the water. The next few hours were some of the most arduous of my life, and by the time he called it a night and sent me to my cell to rest, I was so tired that I collapsed halfway there and had to be carted back to my hammock by a couple of sympathetic guards.

CHAPTER FOUR

I WAS SO STIFF when I woke that I thought I wouldn't be able to make it to the maze, let alone find my way out of it! But after a couple of minutes of walking around, I worked off the stiffness and felt as fit as ever. I realized Vanez had pushed me exactly the right amount and made a note not to doubt his tactics in the future.

I was hungry, but Vanez had told me not to eat anything when I woke — if things were tight, a few extra pounds could mean the difference between living and dying.

Mr. Crepsley and Vanez came for me when it was time. Both wore their best clothes, Mr. Crepsley dazzling in bright red robes, Vanez less flamboyant in a dull brown tunic and trousers.

"Ready?" Vanez asked. I nodded. "Hungry?"

"Starving!"

"Good." He smiled. "I'll treat you to the finest meal of your life after the Trial. Think about that if you get into trouble — it helps to have something to look forward to."

We wound our way down through the torch-lit tunnels to the Aquatic Maze, Vanez walking in front of me, Mr. Crepsley and Harkat just behind. Vanez carried a purple flag, the sign that he was escorting a vampire to a Trial. Most of the vampires we passed made a strange gesture when they saw me coming: they put the tip of their right-hand middle finger to their forehead, placed the tips of the fingers on either side of it on their eyelids, and spread their thumb and little finger out wide to the sides.

"Why are they doing that?" I asked Vanez.

"It's a customary gesture," he explained. "We call it the death's touch sign. It means, 'Even in death, may you be triumphant.'"

"I'd rather they just said good luck," I muttered.

"That doesn't have quite the same significance," Vanez chuckled. "We believe that the gods of the vampires respect those who die nobly. They bless us when a vampire meets death proudly and curse us when one dies poorly."

"So they want me to die well for their own sakes," I said sarcastically.

"For the sake of the clan," Vanez corrected me seriously. "A vampire in good standing always puts the good of the clan before his own well-being. Even in death. The hand gesture is to remind you of that."

The Aquatic Maze was built in the pit of a large cavern. From the top it looked like a long square box. Around the sides of the pit were forty or fifty vampires, the most the cave could hold. Among them were Gavner and Kurda, Seba Nile and Arra Sails — and Mika Ver Leth, the Vampire Prince who'd sentenced me to the Trials.

Mika summoned us over, nodded gravely to Vanez and Mr. Crepsley, then fixed his icy gaze on me. He was dressed in his customary black outfit and looked even sterner than Mr. Crepsley. "You have prepared for the Trial?" he asked.

"I have."

"You know what lies ahead of you?"

"I do."

"Except for the four exits, there is no escape from the maze," he said. "Should you fail this Trial, you will not have to face the Hall of Death."

"I'd rather die at the stakes to drowning," I grunted.

"Most vampires would," he agreed. "But you don't need to worry — it is still water, not running."

I frowned. "What's that got to do with anything?"

"Still water cannot trap a vampire's soul," he explained.

"Oh, that old myth," I laughed. Many vampires believed that if you died in a river or stream, your soul remained trapped forever by the flowing water. "That doesn't bother me. It's the drowning I don't like!"

"Either way, I wish you luck," Mika said.

"No, you don't." I sniffed.

"Darren!" Mr. Crepsley said.

"It's all right." Mika silenced him with a wave of his hand. "Let the boy speak his mind."

"*You* made me take the Trials," I said. "You don't think I'm good enough to be a vampire. You'll be happy if I fail, because it'll prove you were right."

"Your assistant has a low opinion of me, Larten," Mika remarked.

"He is young, Mika. He does not know his place."

"Don't apologize for him. The young *should* speak their minds." He addressed me directly again. "You are right in one thing only, Darren Shan — I *don't* think you have what it takes to make it as a vampire. As for the rest of what you say . . ." — He shook his head — "No vampire takes pleasure in seeing another fail. I sincerely hope you prove me wrong. We need vampires in good standing, now more than ever. I will raise a glass of blood to your name if you complete the Trials, and willingly admit in public that I misjudged you."

"Oh," I said, confused. "In that case, I guess I'm sorry for what I said. No hard feelings?"

The black-haired, eagle-eyed Prince smiled tightly. "No hard feelings." Then he clapped his hands loudly and barked sharply, "May the gods bless you with the luck of the vampires!" — and the Trial began.

I was blindfolded, placed on a stretcher, and carried into the heart of the maze by four guards — so I couldn't memorize the way. Once inside, I was set down and the blindfold was removed. I found myself in a narrow corridor, about five feet wide, less than six and a half feet high. My size would work in my favor in this Trial — tall vampires had to stoop, which made the going even harder.

"Are you ready?" one of the guards asked.

"I'm ready," I said, glancing around the corridor to find my first marker. I saw a whitish stone in the wall to my left and made note of it, starting my mental map-making process.

"You must stay here till the water pours," the guard said. "That's the signal for the start of the Trial. Nobody can check on you once we leave, so there's nothing to prevent you from cheating, apart from your conscience."

"I won't cheat," I snapped. "I'll wait for the water."

"I'm sure you will," the vampire smiled apologetically. "I had to say it anyway — tradition."

The four guards gathered up the stretcher and left. They were all wearing extrasoft shoes, so their footsteps made no noise.

Small candles were set in glass bulbs in the roof of the maze, so I'd have plenty of light to see by, even when the water rose high.

My nerves gnawed at me while I was waiting for the water to gush. A cowardly voice inside my head nudged me to make an early start. Nobody would ever know. Better to live with a little shame than die because of stupid pride.

I ignored the voice — I'd never be able to look Mr. Crepsley, Gavner, or the others in the eye if I cheated.

Finally there was a gurgling sound, and water bubbled up out of a nearby pipe. Breathing a sigh of relief, I hurried for the end of the corridor, dragging my rock behind me, shaking the rope at regular intervals, as Vanez had taught me.

I made good time at the beginning. The water barely held me back, and there were plenty of striking stones to identify the different corridors by. I didn't panic when I came to a dead end or worked my way back to a corridor I'd already visited; I just stuck my head down and kept walking, taking a new route.

The going got tough after five or six minutes. The water was up above my knees. Each step was an effort. The rock now felt as if it weighed a ton. I was having trouble breathing, and my muscles ached, especially in my legs and back.

Still I didn't panic. Vanez had prepared me for this. I had to accept the water, not fight it. I let my pace drop. The mistake many vampires made was to try walking quickly — they exhausted themselves early and never got anywhere near the end.

Another couple of minutes passed. I was growing anxious. There was no way to tell how close or far from the finish I was. I could be a single turn away from an exit door without knowing it — or nowhere near one. At least I'd recognize an exit if I saw it — a huge white X was painted on all four doors and a large black button was in the center of the X. All I had to do was press that button, and the door would open, the water would flood out, and I'd be safe.

The trouble was finding it. The water was up to my

chest by this point, and the rock was getting heavier all the time. I'd stopped shaking the rope — it was too much of an effort — and could feel it drifting along behind me, threatening to get caught between my legs. That happened sometimes — vampires got knotted up in the rope and came to a standstill, drowning where they stood.

I was turning a corner when the rock snagged on something. I gave the rope a pull, trying to free it — with no luck. Taking a deep breath, I dived down to see what was wrong. I found that the rock had jammed against a large crack in a wall. It only took a few seconds to pry it loose, but when I sprang up, I suddenly realized that my mind was a blank. Had I been in this tunnel before? I looked for a familiar sign, but couldn't see any. There was a yellow stone high up in one of the walls, and I thought I'd passed it earlier, but I didn't know for sure.

I was lost!

I lurched to the end of the corridor, then up another, desperately trying to establish my position. Panic flooded my system. I kept thinking, "I'm going to drown! I'm going to drown!" I could have passed a dozen markers and not recognized any of them, I was so stressed out.

The water was up to my chin. It splashed into my

mouth. Sputtering, I slapped at the water, as though that would make it go away. I stumbled and fell. Came up spitting water and gasping. Terrified, I started to scream . . .

. . . and that stopped me. The sound of my roars snapped me back to my senses. I remembered Vanez's advice, stood perfectly still, shut my eyes, and refused to budge until I had the panic under control. I concentrated on the thought of the feast that awaited me. Fresh meat, wild roots, and fruit. A bottle of human blood to perk me up. Dessert — mountain berries, hot and juicy.

I opened my eyes. My heart had stopped beating like a drum, and the worst of the panic attack had passed. I waded slowly down the corridor, searching for a marker. If I could find one, I was sure I'd recall the rest of my mental map. I reached the end of the corridor — no markers. The next corridor was also new to me. And the one after that. And the next.

I could feel the panic bubbling up again when I spotted a candleholder set in a pale grey circular stone — one of my markers! I stared at the candle and waited for my map to reform. For several long seconds my mind remained as terrifyingly blank as it had been — then the map fell back into place. It came to me in sections first, a piece at a time, then in a rush. I stood where I was for a few more seconds, making sure I had it clear in my head before continuing.

The water was up to my lower lip now. The movement was almost impossible. I had to proceed in sluggish jumps, lurching forward to keep my head above water, being extra careful not to bash it on the ceiling. How long before I ran out of air? Three minutes? Four? It couldn't be much more than that. I had to find the way out — and quick!

Concentrating on the map inside my head, I tried figuring out how far away I was from the spot where I'd started. By my calculations, I should be near one of the border walls. If I was, and the exit door was close by, I stood a chance. Otherwise the Trial was as good as over.

Turning a corner, I ran into my first stretch of border wall. I knew it immediately, because the stones were darker and rougher than the rest of the maze. There was no X printed on it, but my heart gave a joyous leap anyway. Backtracking, I banished the map from my thoughts — it was no use to me anymore — and hurried to the next turn, searching for that elusive X.

I found four different sections of border wall, none of which contained the exit. The water was almost up to the ceiling now. I was swimming more than walking, pressing my lips to the ceiling to draw in air. I'd have been OK if it wasn't for the horrible rock — it dragged behind me worse than ever when I tried to swim, slowing me down to a crawl.

As I paused to take a breath, I realized it was time to make a critical decision. Vanez had discussed this with me in the practice maze. He'd hoped things wouldn't reach this stage, but if they did, I had to choose correctly.

If I continued as I was, I'd die. I was making very little progress, and in a minute or two the water would cover my face completely, and I'd drown. The time had come to gamble. One last roll of the dice. If the luck of the vampires was with me, it would mean survival. If not . . .

I took several deep breaths, filling my lungs, then ducked under the water and dived to the floor. Picking up the rock, I turned over, so I was floating on my back, and placed the rock on my belly. Then I swam. It was awkward — streams of water forced themselves up my nose — but this was the only way to stop the rock from dragging me down.

Vampires can hold their breath longer than humans — five or six minutes, easily — but because I was on my back, I had to keep blowing air out through my nose, to stop the water from going up it, so I'd have two, three minutes at most before I ran out of oxygen and drowned.

Swimming around another corner, I stared down a long corridor. I could spot the shape of what must be border wall at the end, but I was too far away to see if there was an X on it or not. I thought there might be, but that could be my mind playing tricks — Vanez had warned me about underwater mirages.

I swam up the corridor. About halfway, I realized there was no X — a long crack in the stones had fooled me — so I turned and quickly headed back the way I'd come. The weight of the rock was forcing me down. I stopped, put my feet on the floor, and used them to push myself up, then straightened out and re-sumed swimming.

I searched in vain for another glimpse of border wall, but the next two corners both led to other corridors, not the wall. My oxygen was running out. It was getting harder and harder to move my arms and legs.

The next turn didn't lead to border wall either, but I had no time to swim ahead and look for another corner. Summoning all of my energy, I swam down the short corridor and took the right turn at the end. That led to another short corridor. As I started down it, the rock slipped off my belly, scratching me as it fell. I yelped without thinking. Water rushed in, and air rushed out.

Coughing, I aimed for the ceiling to draw more air, but when I reached it, I found the water had beaten me to the punch — there was no more air.

I was treading water, silently cursing the fates and vampire gods. This was the end. I'd given it my best, but it wasn't meant to be. The best thing now would be to open my mouth, gulp in water, and make as quick an end of it as I could. I would have too, except this corridor wasn't well lit, and I didn't like the idea of dying in darkness. So, painfully, I dived again to the floor, gathered the rock, turned over onto my back, placed the rock on my belly, and swam ahead to find somewhere brighter to die.

As I made a left turn at the end of the corridor, I spotted the dark stone of border wall. I smiled weakly, remembering how excited that would have made me a few minutes ago. I rolled over onto my belly, so that I could die on my feet — then stopped.

There was an X on the wall!

I stared at it stupidly while precious air bubbles popped out of my mouth. Was this another trick of my mind? Another false crack? It must be. There was no way I could be this lucky. I should ignore it and . . .

No! It *was* an X!

I was out of air and strength, but the sight of that X gave me a new burst of life. Making use of resources I hadn't known I had, I kicked hard with my legs and shot towards the wall like a bullet. I bumped my head against it, recoiled, then rolled over and studied the large, rough X.

I was so delighted to find the X, I almost didn't think to push the button in its center. What a joke that would have been — to come so far and fail at the very end! But thankfully, I was spared that shame. Of its own accord, my left hand crept out, ran its fingers over the button set in the X, then pressed it. The button slid inwards, and the X vanished as the stone slid back into the wall.

With a huge slushing roar, water gushed out through the gap. I was carried along with it, jolting to a stop just beyond the door when my rock caught on something. My eyes and mouth were shut, and for a while it seemed as if I was still submerged in the maze, as water flooded out over my head. Gradually, though, the water level dropped, and I realized I could breathe.

After the deepest breath of my life, I opened my eyes and blinked. The cavern seemed a lot brighter than it had less than half an hour ago, when I'd been led down to it by Vanez Blane. I felt as if I was sitting on a beach on a warm summer's day.

Cheers and hollers reached my ears. Staring around like a fish on dry land, I noticed delighted vampires streaming towards me, splashing through pools of water, whooping with excitement. I was too tired to identify their faces, but I recognized the orange crop of hair on the vampire leading the way — Mr. Crepsley.

As the water subsided, I struggled to my feet and stood outside the door of the Aquatic Maze, smiling foolishly, rubbing the bump on my head where I'd hit the wall. "You did it, Darren!" Mr. Crepsley roared, reaching my side and throwing his arms around me in a rare display of affection.

Another vampire embraced me and yelled, "I thought you'd had it! So much time had passed, I was sure you'd failed!"

Blinking water from my eyes, I made out the features of Kurda and Gavner. And close behind, Vanez and Arra. "Mr. Crepsley? Kurda? Vanez? What are you doing on a beach in the middle of the day?" I asked. "You'll sizzle in the sunlight if you don't watch out."

"He's delirious!" Someone laughed.

"Who would not be?" Mr. Crepsley replied, hugging me proudly.

"Think I'll sit down awhile," I muttered. "Call me when it's time to build sand castles." And, collapsing on my bottom, I stared up at the roof, convinced it was the wide open sky, and hummed merrily to myself while the vampires fussed around me.

CHAPTER FIVE

I WAS SHIVERING like a bedraggled rat when I woke up late the next day. I'd been asleep for fifteen hours or more! Vanez was there to wish me good morning. He handed me a small mug full of a dark liquid and told me to drink.

"What is it?" I asked.

"Brandy," he said. I hadn't tried brandy before. After the first mouthful, which made me gag, I decided I liked it. "Careful." Vanez laughed as I poured it freely down my throat. "You'll get drunk!"

Laying aside the mug, I hiccuped and grinned. Then I remembered the Trial. "I did it!" I shouted, jumping up. "I found the way out!"

"You certainly did," Vanez agreed. "It was close. You were in there just over twenty minutes. Did you have to swim towards the finish?"

"Yes," I said, then described all that had happened in the maze.

"You performed excellently," Vanez said. "Brains, strength, and luck — no vampire lasts long without a healthy measure of each."

Vanez led me to the Hall of Khledon Lurt to get something to eat. The vampires there applauded when they saw me and crowded around to tell me how well I'd done. I made light of it and acted humble, but inside I felt like a hero. Harkat Mulds turned up while I was digging into my third bowl of bat broth and fifth slice of bread. "I am . . . glad you . . . survived," he said in his simple, direct fashion.

"Me too," I laughed.

"The betting . . . against you . . . has dropped . . . since you passed . . . the first Trial. More vampires . . . are betting . . . on you to . . . win, now."

"That's good to hear. Have *you* bet anything on me?"

"I have . . . nothing to bet," Harkat said. "If I did . . . I would."

While we were talking, a rumor spread through the Hall, upsetting the vampires around us. Listening closely, we learned that one of the last remaining vampires on his way to Council had arrived before dawn and immediately rushed to the Hall of Princes to in-form them of vampaneze tracks he'd come across while traveling to the mountain.

"Maybe it's the same vampaneze we found on our way here," I said, referring to a dead vampaneze we'd stumbled on during the course of our journey.

"Maybe," Vanez muttered, unconvinced. "I'll leave you for a while. Stay here. I won't be long."

When he returned, the games master seemed worried. "The vampire was Patrick Goulder," he said. "He came by an entirely different route, and the tracks were quite fresh. It's almost certain that this was a different vampaneze."

"What does it mean?" I asked, unsettled by the anxious rumblings of the vampires around us.

"I don't know," Vanez admitted. "But two vampaneze on the paths to Vampire Mountain are hardly coincidence. And when you take Harkat's message about the Vampaneze Lord into consideration, it doesn't look promising."

I thought again of Harkat's message and Mr. Tiny's long-ago vow that the Vampaneze Lord would lead the vampaneze against the vampires and crush them. I'd had other things to worry about, and still did — my Trials were far from over — but it was hard to ignore this ominous threat to the entire vampire clan.

"Still," Vanez said, making light of it, "the doings

of the vampaneze are of no interest to us. We must concentrate on the Trials. We'll leave the other business to those best equipped to deal with it."

But try as we might to avoid the topic, the rumors followed us around the Halls all day long, and my achievements of the night before went unmentioned — nobody was interested in the fate of a single half-vampire while the future of the race itself hung in the balance.

Hardly anyone paid attention to me when I turned up with Vanez Blane at the Hall of Princes at dusk. A few pressed their right-hand fingers to their forehead and eyelids when they saw the purple flag — the death's touch sign — but they were too preoccupied to discuss my first Trial with me. We had to wait a long time for the Princes to beckon us forward — they were arguing with their Generals, trying to decide what the vampaneze were up to and how many might be skulking around. Kurda was standing up for his outcast friends.

"If they meant to attack us," he shouted, "they would have done so on the trail, while we were coming singly or in pairs."

"Maybe they plan to attack us on the way back," someone retorted.

"Why should they?" Kurda challenged him. "They've never attacked before. Why start now?"

"Perhaps the Vampaneze Lord put them up to it," an old General suggested, and nervous growls of agreement echoed around the Hall.

"Nonsense!" Kurda snorted. "I don't believe those old legends. Even if they *are* true, Mr. Tiny said the night of his coming *was at hand* — not already upon us."

"Kurda is correct," Paris Skyle said. "Besides, attacking us in such a fashion — alone, on our way to or from Council — would be cowardly, and the vampaneze are no cowards."

"They why are they here?" someone cried. "What are they up to?"

"It's possible," Kurda said, "that they came to see *me*."

Every vampire in the Hall stared at him.

"Why should they do that?" Paris asked.

"They are my friends." He sighed. "I don't believe this Vampaneze Lord myth, but many vampaneze do, and a lot are as troubled by it as we are — they don't want a war any more than we do. It's possible that Mr. Tiny sent word to the vampaneze as he did to us, and the pair found on the way here were coming to warn me, or to discuss the situation."

"But Patrick Goulder couldn't find the second vampaneze," Mika Ver Leth said. "If he's still alive, wouldn't he have contacted you by now?"

"How?" Kurda asked. "A vampaneze can't waltz up to the gates and ask for me by name. He'd be killed on sight. If he is a messenger, he's probably waiting somewhere nearby, hoping to catch me when I leave."

That made sense to a lot of vampires, but others dismissed it out of hand — the idea of a vampaneze going out of his way to help a vampire was lunacy as far as they were concerned — and the argument reared up again and bubbled on for another couple of hours.

Mr. Crepsley said little during the arguing. He just sat in his pew near the front, listening carefully, thinking hard. He was so absorbed in what was being said, he hadn't even noticed my arrival.

Finally, during a lull, Vanez crept forward and whispered to one of the guards, who advanced to the platform and spoke in the ear of Paris Skyle (his only good ear — his right had been chopped off many years before). Paris nodded, then clapped loudly for silence. "We have been overlooking our duties, my friends," he said. "The news of the vampaneze is worrying, but we must not let it interfere with regular Council affairs. There is a young half-vampire for whom time is precious. May we enjoy a few minutes of peace to deal with his more pressing concerns?"

When the vampires had settled back into their seats, Vanez escorted me up to the platform.

"Congratulations on passing the first of your Trials, Darren," Paris said.

"Thank you," I replied politely.

"As one who never learned to swim, I have extra reason to admire your narrow escape," said Arrow, the large, bald Prince, with tattoos of arrows on his arms and head. "Had I found myself in your position, I wouldn't have made it out alive."

"You did well, young Shan," Mika Ver Leth agreed. "A good start is half the battle. There's a long way to go, but I'm willing to accept that I might have been wrong about you."

"We would hear about more of your exploits in the maze if we had the time," Paris sighed, "but, alas, that is a tale you must save for another occasion. Are you ready to choose your next Trial?"

"I am."

The bag of numbered stones was produced. After

they'd been checked, I reached in, dug down, and picked one close to the bottom. "Number twenty-three," the guard called out, having examined the stone. "The Path of Needles."

"I thought there were only seventeen Trials," I muttered to Vanez as the stone was taken to the Princes.

"Seventeen for you," he agreed, "but there are more than sixty in total. A lot have been omitted because they're not currently possible to host — like the pit of snakes — and others have been left out because of your size and age."

"Is it a difficult Trial?" I asked.

"It's easier than the Aquatic Maze," he said. "And your size will help. It's as good as any we could have hoped for."

The Princes examined the stone, announced their approval, then set it aside and wished me well. They'd treated me rather curtly, but I understood their distraction and didn't feel slighted. As Vanez and I left, I heard the arguments about the vampaneze kick into life again, and the thick air of tension in the Hall was almost as suffocating as the water in the Aquatic Maze had been.

CHAPTER SIX

THE PATH of Needles was a long, narrow cavern filled with sharp-tipped stalactites and stalagmites. Vanez took me to see it before we set off to practice in another cave.

"All I have to do is walk across?" I asked.

"That's all."

"It isn't much of a Trial, is it?" I said confidently.

"We'll see if you think the same way tomorrow," he grunted. "The stalagmites are slippery — one wrong move and you can impale yourself in the flicker of an eye. And many of the stalactites are precariously perched, hanging by a thread. Any sudden noise will result in some falling. If one hits you on the way down, it can cut clean through you."

Despite his warning, I still felt it was going to be

easy. But by the end of our first practice session, I'd changed my mind.

We practiced in a cave where the stalagmites weren't as sharp or as slippery as those on the Path of Needles, where the stalactites wouldn't break off and fall without warning. Yet, mild as this cave was in comparison, I came close to spearing myself several times, rescued only by the quick hands of Vanez Blane.

"You're not gripping hard enough!" he growled after I'd almost gouged an eye out. I'd scratched my cheek on the stalagmite, and Vanez was applying spit to the cut, to stop the flow of blood (as a half-vampire, my spit was no good for closing cuts).

"It's like trying to hold on to a buttered pole," I grumbled.

"That's why you must grip harder."

"But it hurts. I'll cut my hands to shreds if I —"

"Which would you rather?" Vanez interrupted. "Bloody hands or a stalagmite through your heart?"

"That's a stupid question," I groaned.

"Then stop acting stupidly!" he snapped. "You'll cut your palms to ribbons on the Path of Needles — there's no way to avoid that. You're a half-vampire, so the flesh will grow back quickly. You have to ignore the pain and focus on your grip. There will be plenty of time after the Trial to moan about your poor little fingers and how you'll never play the piano again."

"I can't play the piano anyway," I huffed, but did as he ordered and took a firmer grip on the treacherous mineral stakes.

At the end of the session, Vanez applied special herbs and leaves to my hands, to ease the worst of the pain and toughen up my palms for the ordeal ahead. It felt for a while as though my fingers were on fire, but gradually the pain seeped away, and by the time I had to report back for my second bout of training, it was just a dull throb at the end of my arms.

We concentrated on stealth this time. Vanez taught me to check each stalagmite before transferring my weight onto it. If one snapped off in the cave, it could send me plummeting to my death, or the sound could result in falling stalactites, which were just as hazardous.

"Keep one eye on the ceiling," Vanez said. "Most falling stalactites can be avoided by simply twisting out of the way."

"What if they can't be avoided?" I asked.

"Then you're in trouble. If one's coming for you and can't be dodged, you have to knock it sideways or catch it. Catching is harder but preferable — if you knock a stalactite out of the way, it'll crash and shatter. That sort of noise can bring the roof down."

"I thought you said this was going to be easier than the Aquatic Maze," I complained.

"It is," he assured me. "You need lots of luck to make it out of the Aquatic Maze. On the Path of Needles, you can exert more control over your fate — your life's in your own hands."

Arra Sails turned up during our third practice session, to help me work on my balance. She blindfolded me and made me crawl over a series of blunt stalagmites, so that I learned to maneuver by touch alone. "He has an excellent sense of balance," she noted to Vanez. "As long as he doesn't flinch from the pain in his hands, he should sail through this test."

Finally, after many hours of practice, Vanez sent me back to my cell to grab some shut-eye. Once again he'd worked me just the right amount. Tired, bruised, and cut though I was, after a few hours in my hammock I felt as good as new and ready for anything.

There were hardly any vampires present at the Path of Needles to observe my second Trial. Most were locked away in the Hall of Princes, or had gathered in one of the mountain's many meeting chambers, to discuss the vampaneze. Mr. Crepsley turned out to cheer me on, and so did Gavner Purl and Seba Nile. But Harkat was the only other familiar face in the tiny crowd of well-wishers.

A guard told me that the Princes sent their apologies, but they couldn't preside over the Trial. Vanez complained — he said the Trial should be delayed if a Prince wasn't present — but the guard cited a couple of past cases where Princes hadn't been able to attend Trials, which had gone ahead without them. Vanez asked me if I wanted to push the point — he said, if we created a fuss, we could probably persuade the Princes to postpone the Trial for a night or two, till one of them had time to come down and watch — but I said I'd rather get it over with.

The guard who'd been sent by the Princes checked to make sure I knew what I had to do, wished me luck, guided me to the mouth of the Path of Needles, and set me loose.

I climbed up onto the first of the stalagmites and stared at the sea and sky of glinting spikes. The cavern was well named — from this point it looked precisely like a pathway built of needles. Suppressing a shiver, I started ahead at a snail's crawl. There was no rushing on the Path of Needles. To survive, you had to move slowly and surely. I tested each stalagmite before choosing it, shaking it gently from side to side, making sure it would hold my weight.

Bringing up my legs was tricky. There was no way to grip the tips of the stalagmites with my toes, so I had to place my feet lower down, sometimes wedging them between two stalagmites. While this gave me a chance to take the weight off my arms and hands, it resulted in lots of scratching to my knees and thighs when it came time to drag my legs forward.

It was worst in the spots where the stalactites hung low over the stalagmites. There, I had to stretch out, so that I was lying almost flat on the stalagmites, in order to wriggle ahead. I picked up many nasty cuts to my chest, belly, and back. After a while I found myself envying those fabulous Indian fakirs who can train themselves to lie on a bed of nails!

About a fifth of the way in, my left leg slipped and banged loudly against one of the stalagmites. There was a trembling, tingling sound overhead. Glancing up, I saw several nearby stalactites shaking. For a couple of seconds it seemed as if they weren't going to fall, but then one snapped free and shattered on the ground. The noise of that shook others loose, and suddenly stalactites were dropping like nail bombs all around me.

I didn't panic. Thankfully, hardly any of the stalactites fell close enough to damage me. One would have cut my right arm in two if I hadn't spotted it and shifted out of the way, and I had to suck my gut in quickly to avoid a small but sharp stalactite from ripping a new belly button in my middle. But otherwise I stayed perched where I was, watching the ceiling closely for signs of danger, and waited out the avalanche.

Eventually the stalactites stopped falling, and the echoes of their shattering died away. I waited a minute, for fear of late droppers — Vanez had warned me about those — but when all looked safe I proceeded at my same cautious pace.

The falling stalactites had taken my mind off my torn, pricked body. Adrenaline had surged through me when I saw the shower of lethal needles, and I was temporarily immune to pain. Sensation returned the farther I progressed, but I remained numb to most of the cuts, only wincing every now and then when an especially sharp point bit deeper into my flesh than usual.

I got a good grip with my feet at the halfway point and rested for five or six minutes. The ceiling was high here, so I was able to stand up and rotate my arms and neck, working some of the stiffness out of my muscles.

It was hot and I was sweating like crazy. I was wearing a tight leather outfit, which made me sweat even worse but which was necessary — loose clothes would have snagged on the stalactites.

Many vampires wore no clothes when going through the Path of Needles, but although I hadn't minded stripping to get through a valley full of sharp thorns on the way to Vampire Mountain, I wasn't about to take my clothes off in front of a bunch of strangers!

I wiped my hands on my pants, but they were so stained with blood by this point that my hands became slippier than they'd been before. Looking around, I found a few pockets of dirt and used the dust to dry my palms. The dirt got in under my torn flesh and stung as if I'd grabbed two fistfuls of prickers, but the pain subsided after a while and I was ready to continue.

I was making good time and had passed the three-quarters point when I made my first real mistake. Though the ceiling was high in this part of the cavern, the stalagmites grew close together, and I had to stretch out to crawl over them. The tips were digging into my belly and chest, so I picked up speed, anxious to clear the vicious cluster.

Reaching ahead with my left hand, I tested a large stalagmite, but only slightly — it was so big, I felt sure it would support me. As I shifted my weight onto it, there was a sharp cracking sound, and the tip broke away in my hand. I realized immediately what was happening and tried retreating, but it was too late. My weight had snapped the tip clean off, and my body dipped, slamming into a few neighboring stalagmites.

The noise wasn't especially loud, but it built like thunder, and I could hear familiar tingling sounds overhead. Easing my head around, I glued my eyes to the ceiling and watched as several small stalactites fell and smashed. They didn't bother me — even if they'd been on target, they couldn't have done much harm — but the enormous stalactite directly above caused my guts to shrivel in fearful anticipation. For a while it looked like I was safe — the initial noise didn't even make the stalactite quiver — but, as smaller stalactites dropped and exploded, the larger one began to shake, gently at first, then alarmingly.

I tried scurrying out of its way, but I was snagged on the stalagmites. It would take a few seconds to free myself. I half rolled over, creating room to maneuver. I was staring up at the stalactite, judging how long I had to wriggle clear, when I thought about the stalactites around it. If the big one fell and smashed, the vibrations would bring pretty much every stalactite in this part of the cavern down on top of me!

While I was considering the problem and trying to figure a way out of it, the large stalactite snapped abruptly in the middle, and the lower half dropped upon me in a rush, its pin-sharp tip directed like an arrow at the soft flesh of my belly — it was going to go right through me!

CHAPTER SEVEN

I HAD A SPLIT SECOND to think and react. For a human, it would have been all over. As a half-vampire, I stood a chance. Wriggling out of the way was impossible — no time — so I flopped onto my back, bracing myself against the flat rim of the stalagmite whose tip I'd broken off. Letting go of the stalagmites around me, ignoring the pain as a dozen sharp tips dug into me, I raised my hands above my body and grabbed for the dropping stalactite.

I caught it in midair, several inches above the tip. It slid down through my hands, shedding tiny silver splinters all along the flesh of my palms. I had to bite down hard on my tongue to hold an agonized yell inside.

Ignoring the pain, I pressed my hands closer together, gripping the stalactite as tightly as I could, and the tip came to a stop a couple of inches above my belly. The muscles in my arms creaked at the effort it took to stop and hold the heavy piece of stalactite, but didn't let me down.

Gently, with trembling arms, I laid the stalactite to one side, careful not to make any noise, then lifted myself off the stalagmites and blew on my bleeding palms, the lines of which had been severed in dozens of places by the sharp sides of the stake. By the luck of the vampires, none of my fingers had been amputated, but that was the only thing I had to feel grateful for.

The rest of my body had been similarly lacerated. I felt like I'd been stabbed all over. Blood was flowing freely from my back, arms, and legs, and I could feel a deep impression in the skin of my lower back, where the rim of the big stalagmite had cut into me.

But I was *alive!*

I took my time going over the rest of the sharp cluster, hard as it was. Once clear, I paused, wiped the blood from my hands, licked my fingers, and rubbed spit into the worst of my wounds. I wasn't able to close cuts like full-vampires could, but the damp saliva eased some of the pain. A few sorry tears crept down my cheeks, but I knew self-pity would get me nowhere, so I wiped them away and told myself to concentrate — I wasn't out of the cavern yet.

I thought about taking off my top and ripping it to

pieces, wrapping the strips around my hands to give me a firmer grip. But that would have been cheating, and the vampire blood in me boiled angrily at the suggestion. Instead, I found more pockets of dirt and used them to dry my blood-stained palms and fingers. I also rubbed lots of dirt into my feet and lower legs, which were slippery with blood that had dripped from my hands.

After a short rest, I continued. It wasn't so hard on this side of the cluster, but I was in such bad shape that it seemed difficult. I proceeded slowly, testing each stalagmite more thoroughly than necessary, taking no chances at all.

Finally, after more than an hour and a half on the Path of Needles — most vampires made it across in less than forty minutes — I crawled out, to be warmly greeted by the few vampires who'd gathered to cheer my success.

"Well?" Vanez asked, throwing a roughly woven towel around my shoulders. "Still think it isn't much of a Trial?"

I glowered at the games master. "If I ever say such a stupid thing again," I told him, "cut out my tongue and sew my lips closed!"

"Come on," he laughed. "We'll wash off that blood and dirt, then get busy with the balms and bandages."

Supported by Vanez and Mr. Crepsley, I hobbled away from the Path of Needles and said a silent prayer that the next Trial would have nothing to do with cramped caverns and razor-sharp obstacles. If I'd known how my prayer was going to be answered, I wouldn't have bothered!

As it turned out, I didn't have to worry about my next Trial immediately. While I was showering under an icy-cold waterfall in the Hall of Perta Vin-Grahl, word reached us that the final vampire had arrived at the mountain, which meant the Festival of the Undead would begin at the end of the next day, with the setting of the sun.

"There!" Vanez beamed. "Three nights and days to drink, be merry, recover, and relax. Things couldn't have worked out better if we'd planned them."

"I don't know," I groaned, using my fingernails to dig dirt out of the cuts in my legs and feet. "I think I'll need a couple of weeks — at least!"

"Nonsense," Vanez said. "A few nights and you'll be good as new. A little scarred and scratched, but nothing that will work against you in the later Trials."

"Will I have my extra allotted day to prepare for

the Trial, on top of the three days allowed for the Festival?" I asked.

"Of course," he said. "There can be no official business during the Festival of the Undead. It's a time for rest and games and the swapping of old tales. Even the subject of the vampaneze must be put on ice for the next three nights and days.

"I've been looking forward to this for months," Vanez said, rubbing his hands together. "As a games master, I can have nothing to do with organizing or overseeing games during the Festival — so I can cut loose and really enjoy myself, without having to worry about what others are getting up to."

"Can you take part in the games with just one eye?" I asked.

"Certainly," he replied. "There are a few which require the use of both, but most don't. Wait and see — I'll crack many a head before the final ceremonies of the Festival. Dozens of vampires are going to leave the Council cursing my name and the night they crossed me."

When I finished showering, I stepped out of the waterfall and wrapped myself in several towels. I stood by a couple of strong torches to dry out, then Vanez bandaged the worst of my wounds, and I slipped into the light clothes he'd provided. Although the material was wafer thin, I felt uncomfortable, and as soon as I was back in my cell I got rid of the clothes and lay down naked in my hammock.

I didn't get much sleep that night — I was too sore. Though I tried to lie still, I couldn't, and my tossing and turning kept me awake. Finally I got up, pulled on a pair of pants, and went looking for Harkat. It turned out he was back in the Hall of Princes — they were questioning him about his message from Mr. Tiny one last time, before the Festival of the Undead — so I returned to my cell, found a mirror, and passed a few hours counting the scratches on the backs of my arms and legs.

As day came — I was getting used to the passage of time inside the mountain; when I'd first arrived I hadn't been able to tell the difference between day and night — I got back in my hammock and tried to sleep again. This time I managed to doze off, and though my sleep was fitful, I squeezed in a handful of hours before the start of the much-awaited Festival of the Undead.

CHAPTER EIGHT

THE FESTIVAL got under way in the immense Hall of Stahrvos Glen (also known as the Hall of Gathering). Every vampire in the mountain was present. Large as the Hall was, we were squeezed in like sardines. Looking around while we waited for sunset, I counted at least four hundred heads, possibly as many as five.

Everyone was dressed up in brightly colored clothes. The few female vampires in the Hall wore long, flowing dresses, and most of the men wore handsome (but dusty) capes. Mr. Crepsley and Seba Nile wore matching red costumes and looked like father and son as they stood side by side. Even Harkat had borrowed new bright blue robes for the occasion.

I was the only one who looked out of place. I was itching like mad from my cuts and scratches and was wearing the dull, thin shirt and pants that Vanez had given me in the Hall of Perta Vin-Grahl. Even that flimsy material irritated me — I kept reaching back and plucking it off my skin. Mr. Crepsley told me several times to stop fidgeting, but I couldn't.

"Come see me later," Seba whispered as I tugged at my shirt for the thousandth time. "I have something which will ease much of the itching."

I started to thank the old quartermaster, but a gong sounded loudly and cut me off. Every vampire in the Hall stopped talking at the ringing of the gong. Moments later the three Vampire Princes appeared at the head of the Hall and mounted a platform so that all could see them clearly. The Festival of the Undead and the Ceremony of Conclusion — which would come at the end of Council — were the only times that all the Princes left their impregnable Hall at the top of the mountain. At least one of them was always present the rest of the time.

"It is good to see you, my friends." Paris Skyle beamed.

"We welcome you all to Vampire Mountain," Mika Ver Leth said.

"And wish you well during your stay," Arrow added.

"I know all of you have heard the rumors of the vampaneze," Paris said. "These are troubling times, and there is much to discuss and plan. But not during these next three nights. Because this is the Festival of the Undead, where every vampire is equal, and all must enjoy themselves."

"I'm sure everyone's eager to get the festivities rolling," Mika said. "But first the roll call of those who've passed on to Paradise since last we met for Council."

Arrow called out the names of nine vampires who'd died during the past twelve years. As each name was announced, the vampires in the Hall made the death's touch sign and muttered in unison, "Even in death, may he be triumphant."

When the last name had been called, Paris clapped his hands and said, "That is the last piece of official business out of the way. There shall be no more until the close of the Festival. Luck to you, my friends."

"Luck!" the vampires shouted, and then they were tossing their capes off, roughly hugging each other, and hollering at the tops of their voices, "Luck! Luck! Luck!"

The next several hours were so exciting, I almost managed to forget about my cuts and the itching. I was swept along to the gaming Halls by a wave of vampires eager to test themselves against old friends and foes. Some couldn't wait to reach the Halls and began wrestling and boxing in the tunnels on the way. They were kept apart by more level-headed vampires and carried — often struggling and protesting — down to the Halls, where they could fight in comfort and for the benefit of an audience.

It was chaos in the three gaming Halls. Because none of the official games masters were on duty, there was nobody to bark commands or make sure everything proceeded in an orderly fashion. Vampires spilled around the Hall and over one another, challenging anyone who got in their way, lashing out joyfully.

Mr. Crepsley was no better than the rest. His usual dignity disappeared in the mad rush, and he ran around like a wild man, yelling, throwing punches, and leaping around. Even the Vampire Princes joined in the madness, including Paris Skyle, who was eight hundred years old.

I bobbed along as well as I could, trying to keep my head above the sea of writhing vampires. The initial burst of crazy activity had scared me a little — I hadn't been expecting it — but I was soon having great fun, dodging between the legs of tussling vampires and knocking them over.

At one point I found myself back-to-back with Harkat. He'd been caught up in the rush with the rest of us and was busy tossing vampires over his shoulders, left and right, as if they were bags of cotton. The vampires loved it — they couldn't understand how someone so little could be so strong — and were lining up to test themselves against him.

I had a chance to catch my breath while I was standing behind Harkat — nobody was interested in a half-vampire when there was a Little Person to challenge. Once I'd recovered some of my spent energy, I slid away and rejoined the throng of battling vampires.

Gradually the chaos died down. A lot of vampires had been injured in the fighting, and while they dragged themselves away to be patched up, those left standing paused to wipe the sweat from their brows and quench their thirst with a good long drink.

After a while the games started for real. Vampires took to the mats, wrestling rings, and bars, two or three at a time, the way they were meant to. Those too tired or too wounded to fight gathered around the sparring vampires and cheered them on.

I watched Mr. Crepsley fighting. It was some form of karate, and he was red-hot at it. His hands moved like lightning, fast even for a vampire, and he knocked down his opponents like flies, usually in a matter of seconds.

At another mat, Vanez was wrestling. The one-eyed games master was having the great time he'd predicted. While I was in attendance, he sent three vampires away with bloody noses and spinning heads, and was making short work of his fourth as I left.

I was passing a jousting ring when a laughing vampire grabbed me and pushed me forward to compete. I didn't protest — it was a law of the Festival that you never refused a challenge. "What are the rules?" I asked, shouting to be heard.

"See the two ropes hanging from the overhead bar?" the vampire who'd dragged me in asked. I nodded. "Grab one and stand on the platform on this side. Your opponent grabs the other and faces you. Then you swing out into the middle and kick and punch each other till one of you gets knocked off."

My opponent was a large, hairy vampire who looked like a monster out of a comic book. I didn't stand a chance against him, but I gave it a try. Taking a firm hold of the rope, I swung out to meet him and spent a few seconds avoiding his thrashing feet and fist. I managed to kick him in the ribs and slap him around the head, but my blows had no effect, and he soon hit me square in the jaw and swatted me to the floor.

The vampires around the ring rushed forward to

help me up. "Are you OK?" the one who'd volunteered me for the contest asked.

"Fine," I said, checking my teeth with my tongue to see if any were broken. "Is it the best out of three or five?"

The vampires cheered and slapped me on the back — they loved a fighter. I was led back to the rope and went head to head with the gorilla again. I only lasted a few seconds, but nobody expected anything different. I was carried away like a champion and handed a mug of beer. I didn't like the taste, but it would have been rude to refuse, so I drained the glass, smiled as they cheered again, then wobbled away to look for a place to sit down and rest.

A lot of beer, wine, whiskey, and brandy was being consumed (as well as plenty of blood!), but hardly any vampires got drunk. This was because vampires have stronger metabolisms than humans. The average vampire has to drink a whole barrel of beer before he gets tipsy. As a half-vampire, I wasn't as immune to the effects of alcohol as the rest. I felt quite light-headed after my mug of beer and made up my mind not to drink any more — at least not tonight!

Kurda joined me while I was resting. He was flushed and smiling. "Crazy, isn't it?" he said. "All these vampires, acting like wild children. Think how embarrassing it would be if anyone saw us!"

"It's fun though, isn't it?" I laughed.

"Certainly," he agreed. "I'm just glad I only have to endure it once every twelve years."

"Kurda Smahlt!" someone yelled. Looking around, we spotted Arra Sails on her favorite set of bars, twirling a staff over her head. "How about it, Kurda — like your chances?"

Kurda grimaced. "I have a sore leg, Arra," he shouted.

The vampires around the bars jeered.

"Come on, Kurda," Arra called. "Not even a pacifist like you has the right to refuse a challenge during the Festival of the Undead."

Kurda sighed, took of his shoes, and advanced. The vampires gave a roar of delight, and word quickly spread that Kurda Smahlt was going into action against Arra Sails. Soon, a huge crowd had formed around the bars, most of them vampires who wanted to see Kurda end up flat on his back.

"She hasn't been beaten on the bars in eleven years," I murmured to Kurda as he chose his staff.

"I know," he groaned.

"Try not to get too close to her," I advised him (speaking as though I was an expert, when in fact I'd only been on the bars once before). "The more you stay away, the longer you can drag it out."

"I'll bear that in mind."

"And be careful," I warned him. "She'll crack your head right open if you give her the chance."

"Are you trying to *en*courage or *dis*courage me?" he snapped.

"Encourage, of course." I grinned.

"Well, you're doing a lousy job of it!"

He tested a staff, liked the feel of it, and hopped onto the bars. The vampires cheered and moved back, so there'd be plenty of room for him to fall.

"I've been waiting for decades to get you up here." Arra smiled, twirling her staff and advancing.

"I hope it proves worth the wait," Kurda said, blocking her first blow and dancing away from her on the bar.

"You managed to avoid me last time, but there's no escape now. I'm going to —"

Kurda launched a few blows of his own, and Arra leapt backwards, surprised. "Are you here to talk or fight?" Kurda asked pleasantly.

"To fight!" Arra snarled, then concentrated.

The two sparred cautiously for a few minutes, testing each other. Then Arra's staff connected with one of Kurda's knees. It seemed like a mild enough blow, but he teetered on the bar and dropped his guard. Arra grinned and darted forward to finish him off. As she did, Kurda leapt across to a parallel bar and brought his staff around in a broad swing.

Arra was completely taken by surprise, and there was nothing she could do as the staff swept her legs out from under her. She fell to the floor with a thump — *defeated!* There was a stunned silence, then the vampires roared their approval and surged forward to shake Kurda's hand. He thrust through them to check on Arra and see if she was OK. The vampiress slapped his hands away as he bent to help her up.

"Don't touch me!" she seethed.

"I was only trying —," he began.

"You cheated!" she interrupted. "You faked injury. I want to make it the best out of three."

"I beat you fair and square," Kurda said evenly. "There's no rule against faking injury. You shouldn't have leapt in for the kill like you did. If you hadn't been so eager to disgrace me, my trick wouldn't have worked."

Arra glared at the soon-to-be Vampire Prince, then dropped her gaze and muttered, "There is truth in your words." Lifting her eyes, she stared directly at Kurda. "I apologize for insulting you, Kurda Smahlt. I spoke in anger. Will you forgive me?"

"I will if you'll take my hand." Kurda smiled.

Arra shook her head shortly. "I cannot," she said miserably. "You beat me cleanly, and it shames me to refuse your hand — but I cannot bring myself to take it."

Kurda looked hurt, but forced a smile. "That's OK," he said. "I forgive you anyway."

"Thank you," Arra said, then turned and ran from the Hall, her features contorted with the pain of overwhelming shame.

Kurda was heavy-hearted when he sat down beside me. "I feel sorry for her," he sighed. "It must be cruel to be so set in one's ways. Her refusal to shake my hand will haunt her the rest of her life. In her eyes, and the eyes of those who think like her, she's committed an unpardonable act. It doesn't matter much to me whether she shakes my hand or not, but she'll feel she's disgraced herself."

"Nobody could believe it when you beat her," I said, trying to cheer him up. "I thought you weren't supposed to be any good when it came to fighting."

Kurda laughed lightly. "I *choose* not to fight — it doesn't mean I *can't!* I'm no heroic vampire, but I'm not the useless coward many think I am."

"If you fought more often, they wouldn't think that," I noted.

"True," he admitted. "But their opinion doesn't matter." Kurda put his fingers on my chest and pressed softly down on my heart. "In here is where a man should judge himself, not on bars or in a ring or on a battlefield. If you know in your heart that you're true and brave, that should be enough.

"Of the nine vampires who've died since last Council, five could have been here tonight, alive and well, had they not been determined to prove themselves to others. They drove themselves to early graves, just so their companions would admire them." He lowered his head and sighed deeply. "It's stupid," he mumbled. "Pointless and sad. And one night it may prove to be the end of us all."

Rising, he drifted away, sullen and depressed. I sat where I was for a long time after he'd gone, studying the bloodied, battling vampires and mulling over the peaceful Kurda's solemn, troubling words.

CHAPTER NINE

As THE NEW DAY DAWNED most vampires retired to their coffins. They'd have happily continued fighting and drinking, but the first of the formal balls was at sunset, and they had to prepare for it. There'd be three balls during the Festival of the Undead, one at the end of each day. Two large Halls were used for the balls, so all the vampires could fit.

The ball was a strange event. Most of the vampires were dressed in their colorful clothes, as they had been earlier, but now their shirts, pants, and capes were torn, ripped, and blood-stained, while their bodies and faces were scratched and bruised. Many had broken arms and legs, but every single one of them took to the dance floor, even those on crutches.

At the stroke of sunset, the vampires all raised their faces to the ceiling and howled like wild wolves. The howling went on for several minutes, each vampire holding his or her howl as long as possible. They called this the howl of the night, and it was performed at the first ball of each Festival. The aim was to outlast the others — the vampire who held the howl the longest would win the title "of the Howl" and carry it until the following Council. So, if I'd won, I'd have had to be addressed as Darren Shan of the Howl for the next twelve years.

Of course, I didn't come close to winning — since I was only a half-vampire, my voice was one of the weakest, and I was among the first to fall silent. Gradually, as the voices of the others cracked, they fell silent too, one by one, until in the end only a handful were howling, their faces red with the strain of such a fierce bellow. While the last few vampires howled themselves hoarse, the rest urged on their favorites — "Keep it up, Butra!," "Howl like a demon, Yebba!" — and pounded the floor with their feet and hands.

In the end the contest was won by a huge vampire called Yebba. He'd won it twice before — though not at the last Council — and was a popular victor. There was a short ceremony, in which he had to drink a tub of blood straight down without pause, then Paris Skyle dubbed him Yebba of the Howl. Almost as soon as the words had left the Prince's lips, the band began to play, and the vampires started to dance.

The band consisted entirely of drummers, who kept up a slow, heavy beat. As the vampires danced stiffly — short steps, in time with the funereal music — they chanted the words of ancient songs, telling of great battles and vampire champions, praising those who'd died nobly, and cursing those who'd betrayed or shamed the clan (though they didn't name them — it was a custom never to mention the names of traitors or vampires of poor standing).

I tried dancing — everybody had a turn — but I wasn't very good. I could have jumped around to something fast and loud, but this was too precise. If you didn't know how to do it right, you looked stupid. Not knowing any of the words to the somber songs was another drawback. Besides, the dancing made my itching worse than ever, and I kept having to stop to scratch my back.

After a few minutes, I excused myself and slipped away. I went looking for Seba Nile, who'd said he had something that would cure the itching. I found the quartermaster in the second chamber. He was dancing and leading the singing, so I took a seat and waited for him to finish.

Gavner Purl was in the Hall; he spotted me after a while and sat down beside me. He looked exhausted and was breathing heavier than usual. "I only got to my coffin an hour or so ago," he explained. "I was trapped by a couple of my old tutors and had to spend the entire day listening to their stories."

There was a break in the music, while the band drank blood and lined up their next song. Seba bowed to his companions and left the dance floor during the pause. I waved a hand in the air to grab his attention. He stopped to grab a mug of beer, then ambled over. "Gavner. Darren. Enjoying yourselves?"

"I would be if I had the energy," Gavner wheezed.

"How about you, Darren?" Seba asked. "What do you think of our Festival of the Undead?"

"It's weird," I answered honestly. "First you all howl like wild animals — then dance around like robots!"

Seba stifled a laugh. "You should not say such things out loud," he gently chided me. "You will hurt our feelings. Most vampires are proud of their dancing — they think they dance with great style."

"Seba," I said, scratching my legs, "do you remember saying you had something that would stop my itching?"

"I do."

"Would you mind giving it to me now?"

"It is not so easily fetched," Seba said. "We must take a short trip, down to the tunnels beneath the Halls."

"Will you take me when you have the time?" I asked.

"I have the time," he said. "But first find Kurda Smahlt. I promised I would let him accompany me when I next made the trip — he wants to map the region."

"Where should I tell him we're going?" I inquired.

"Tell him we go where the arachnids roam. He will know where I mean. Also, grab that beautiful spider of yours — Madam Octa. I would like to bring her with us."

I found Kurda listening to vampires telling legendary stories from the past. Storytellers were in great demand at the Festival. Vampires didn't bother much with books. They preferred to keep the past alive orally. I don't think the full history of the vampires had ever been written down. I tugged on Kurda's elbow and whispered Seba's message to him. He said he'd accompany us, but asked me to give him a few minutes while he went and collected his mapmaking equipment. He said he'd meet us outside Seba's quarters, low in the mountain, close to the stores that the quartermaster was in charge of.

When I arrived back with Madam Octa, I learned that Gavner had also decided to join us. He thought he'd fall asleep if he stayed where he was, listening to the music, warmed by the glow of the torchers and the press of vampires. "A stroll below decks is just what the captain ordered," he said, imitating a sailor's salty tones.

I looked around for Harkat — I thought he might like to see what the lower tunnels of Vampire Mountain were like — but he was surrounded by admiring vampires. Harkat's metabolism was even stronger than a vampire's, and he could drink alcohol all day and night without being affected. The vampires were astonished by his capacity for drink and were cheering him on as he drank one mug of beer after another. I didn't like to take him away from his newfound friends, so I left him.

When we were ready, we gathered together outside Seba's rooms and set off for the tunnels. The guards at the gate connecting the tunnels to the Halls weren't regular guards — no vampire could carry out his normal duties during the Festival. They weren't dressed as neatly as the regular guards, and some had been drinking, which they'd never do while on duty any other time. Seba told them where we were going, and they waved us through, warning us not to get lost.

"We'd better not." Kurda smirked. "By the smell of you, you'd have trouble finding an apple at the bottom of a barrel of cider!"

The guards laughed and made mock threats not to let us back in. One of the more sober guards asked if we wanted torches, but Seba said we'd be OK — the walls were coated with glowing moss where we were going.

Kurda got his mapmaking equipment out when we reached tunnels where he'd never been before. It was just a sheet of gridded paper and a pencil. He paused every so often to add a tiny piece of line to the page, signifying the length of tunnel we'd traversed.

"Is that all there is to mapmaking?" I asked. "It looks easy."

"Tunnels aren't difficult to map," he agreed. "It's different if you're trying to map open land or a stretch of seacoast."

"Don't listen to him," Gavner said. "Even tunnels are difficult. I tried it once and made a mess of it. You have to work to scale and make sure you mark the length exactly right. If you're off by even the tiniest fraction, it throws the rest of the map off."

"It's just a skill," Kurda said. "You'd pick it up quickly if you gave it a try."

"No, thanks," Gavner said. "I have no intention of spending my spare time trapped down a maze of tunnels, trying to map them out. I don't know what the appeal is."

"It's fascinating," Kurda said. "It gives you a clearer understanding of your environment, not to mention a great sense of achievement when you're finished. Apart from which, there's the practical aspect."

"Practical aspect!" Gavner snorted. "Nobody uses your maps except you!"

"Not so," Kurda corrected him. "Nobody's interested in helping me make maps, but plenty make use of them. Did you know we'll be building a new Hall, lower than any of the other levels, over the next few years?"

"A Hall of storage." Gavner nodded.

"That's being constructed out of a cave *I* discovered, which will connect to the rest of the Halls via a tunnel nobody knew about until *I* went snooping around."

"There are also the breach points," Seba noted.

"What are those?" I asked.

"Tunnels which open into the Halls," Seba explained. "There are many ways into the Halls besides the main gates of entry. Kurda has unearthed many of these and brought them to our attention, so that we might seal them off against attack."

"Who'd attack you up here?" I frowned.

"He's referring to animal attacks," Kurda said. "Stray wolves, rats, and bats often crept in by breach points and went foraging for food. They were getting to be a nuisance. My maps helped put an end to most of their advances."

"OK." Gavner smiled. "I was wrong — your maps *do* serve a purpose. You still wouldn't get me down here helping you make them though."

We proceeded in silence for a while. The tunnels were narrow and the roofs were low-hanging, so it was hard going for the grown vampires. They enjoyed a few minutes of relief when the tunnels opened up briefly, but then they constricted again, and it was back to crouching and shuffling along. It was dark too. We had just enough light to see by, but there wasn't enough for Kurda to make maps. He dug out a candle and started to light it, but Seba stopped him.

"No candles," the quartermaster said.

"But I can't see," Kurda complained.

"I am sorry, but you will have to do the best you can."

Kurda grumbled, bent his head low over the sheet

of paper so his nose was almost touching it, and drew carefully as we progressed, stumbling often because he wasn't watching where he was going.

Finally, after crawling through an especially small tunnel, we found ourselves in a moderately large cave that was coated from floor to ceiling with spiderwebs. "Quiet now," Seba whispered as we stood. "We do not want to disturb the residents."

The "residents" were spiders. Thousands — possibly hundreds of thousands — of them. They filled the cave, dangling from the ceiling, hanging on cobwebs, scuttling across the floor. They were like the spider I'd spotted when I first arrived at Vampire Mountain, hairy and yellow. None was quite as large as Madam Octa, but they were bigger than most ordinary spiders.

A number of the spiders scurried toward us. Seba dropped cautiously to one knee and whistled. The spiders hesitated, then returned to their corners. "Those were sentries," Seba said. "They would have defended the others if we had come to cause trouble."

"How?" I asked. "I thought they weren't poisonous."

"Singly, they are harmless," Seba explained. "But if they attack in groups, they can be dangerous. Death is unlikely — for a human, maybe, but not a vampire —

but certainly severe discomfort occurs, possibly even partial paralysis."

"I see why you wouldn't allow any candles," Kurda said. "One stray spark and this place would go up like dry paper."

"Precisely." Seba wandered into the center of the cave. The rest of us followed slowly. Madam Octa had crept forward to the bars of her cage and was making a careful study of the spiders. "They have been here for thousands of years," Seba whispered, reaching up and letting some of the spiders crawl over his hands and up his arms. "We call them Ba'Halen's spiders, after the vampire who — if the legends are to be believed — first brought them here. No human knows of their existence."

I took no notice as the spiders crept up my legs — I was used to handling Madam Octa, and before her I'd studied spiders as a hobby — but Gavner and Kurda looked uneasy. "Are you sure they won't bite?" Gavner asked.

"I would be surprised if they did," Seba said. "They are gentle and usually only attack when threatened."

"I think I'm going to sneeze," Kurda said as a spider crawled over his nose.

"I would not advise it," Seba warned him. "They might interpret that as an act of aggression."

Kurda held his breath and shook from the effort of controlling the sneeze. His face had turned a bright shade of red by the time the spider moved on. "Let's beat it," he wheezed, letting out a long, shaky breath.

"Best suggestion I've heard all night," Gavner agreed.

"Not so fast, my friends," Seba said with a smile. "I did not bring you here for fun. We are on a mission. Darren — take off your shirt."

"*Here?*" I asked.

"You want to put a stop to the itching, don't you?"

"Well, yes, but . . ." Sighing, I did as Seba ordered. When my back was bare, Seba found some old cobwebs that had been abandoned. "Bend over," he commanded, then held the cobwebs over my back and rubbed them between his fingers, so that they crumbled and sprinkled over my flesh.

"What are you doing?" Gavner asked.

"Curing an itch," Seba replied.

"With cobwebs?" Kurda said skeptically. "Really, Seba, I didn't think you believed in old wives' tales."

"It is no tale," Seba insisted, rubbing the webby ash into my broken skin. "There are chemicals in these cobwebs which aid the healing process and work against irritation. Within an hour, the itching will stop."

When I was covered in ash, Seba tied some thick, whole webs around the worst-infected areas, including my hands. "We will take the webs off before we leave the tunnels," he said, "although I advise against washing for a night or two — the itching may return if you do."

"This is crazy," Gavner muttered. "It'll never work."

"Actually, I think it's working already," I contradicted him. "The backs of my legs were killing me when we came in, but now the itching is barely noticeable."

"If it's so effective," Kurda said, "why haven't we heard about it before?"

"I do not broadcast," Seba said. "If the curative powers of the webs were widely known, vampires would come down here to the caves all the time. They would disturb the natural routines of the spiders, forcing them farther down into the mountain, and within years the supplies would dry up. I only bring people here when they truly need help and always ask them to keep the secret to themselves. I trust none of you will betray my confidence?"

We all said we wouldn't.

Once I'd been taken care of, Seba took Madam Octa out of her cage and set her down on the floor. She squatted uncertainly while a crowd of inquisitive spiders gathered around her. One with light grey spots on its back ducked forward in a testing attack. She swatted it away with ease, and the rest withdrew. Once she'd familiarized herself with the terrain, she explored the cave. She climbed up the walls and onto the cobwebs, disturbing other spiders in the process. They reacted angrily to her intrusion, but calmed down once they saw how large she was and that she meant them no harm.

"They recognize majesty when they see it," Seba noted, pointing to lines of spiders following Madam Octa around. The one with grey spots was in the front. "If we left her here, they would make her a queen."

"Could she breed with them?" Kurda asked.

"Probably not," Seba mused. "But it would be interesting if she could. There has been no new blood introduced to the colony for thousands of years. I would be fascinated to study the offspring of such a union."

"Forget it." Gavner shivered. "What if the babies turned out to be as poisonous as their mother? We'd have thousands of them roaming the tunnels, killing at will!"

"Hardly." Seba smiled. "Spiders tend not to pick

on those bigger than themselves, not while smaller and more vulnerable prey exists. Still, she is not my spider. It is for Darren to decide."

I watched her carefully for a couple of minutes. She looked happy out in the open, among those of her own kind. But I knew better than anyone the awful consequences of her bite. Better not to risk it. "I don't think we should leave her," I said.

"Very well," Seba agreed, pursing his lips and whistling softly. Madam Octa returned to her cage immediately in response, though once inside she kept close to the bars, as though lonely. I felt sorry for her, but reminded myself that she was just a spider and didn't have any real feelings.

Seba played for a while with the spiders, whistling and inviting them to crawl over him. I grabbed the flute — it was really just a fancy tin whistle — from Madam Octa's cage and joined him. It took a few minutes to tune my thoughts into the spiders' — they weren't as easy to make mental contact with as Madam Octa — but Seba and I had fun once I was in control, letting them jump between our bodies and spin adjoining webs that connected us from head to foot.

Gavner and Kurda watched, bemused. "Could I control them too?" Gavner asked.

"I doubt it," Seba said. "It is more difficult than it

looks. Darren is naturally gifted with spiders. Very few people have the ability to bond with spiders. You are a fortunate young man, Darren."

I'd lost enthusiasm for spiders since that nasty business between Madam Octa and my best friend, Steve Leopard, all those years ago, but at Seba's words I felt some of my old love for the eight-legged creatures resurfacing and made myself a promise to take more of an interest in the webby world of spiders in the future.

When we were finished playing, Seba and I brushed off the cobwebs — being careful not to remove the curing webs he'd attached to my body — then the four of us crawled out to the tunnels. Some of the spiders followed us, but turned back when they realized we were leaving, all except the grey-spotted one, which trailed behind us almost to the end of the tunnel, as though in love with Madam Octa and unwilling to see her leave.

CHAPTER TEN

WE'D STARTED back for the Halls when I remembered the old burial site Kurda had told me about not long after I'd arrived at Vampire Mountain. I asked if we could see it. Seba was game and so was Kurda. Gavner wasn't as interested but agreed to tag along. "Burial chambers make me feel gloomy," he said as we wound our way through the tunnels.

"That's an odd view for a vampire," I noted. "Don't you sleep in a coffin?"

"Coffins are different," Gavner said. "I feel snug in a coffin. It's graveyards, morgues, and crematoriums I can't stand."

The Hall of Final Voyage was a large cave with a domed roof. Glowing moss grew thickly on the walls. A stream cut through the middle of the cave and exited via a tunnel that led it back underground. The stream was wide, fast, and loud. We had to raise our voices to be heard above its roar as we stood at its edge.

"The bodies of the dead used to be carried down here," Kurda said. "They were stripped, placed in the water, and let loose. The stream swept them away, through the mountain and out to the wilderness beyond."

"What happened to them then?" I asked.

"They washed up on some far-off bank, where their bodies were devoured by animals and birds of prey." He chuckled when I turned pale. "Not a pretty way to go, is it?"

"It is as good as any," Seba disagreed. "When *I* die, this is how I want to be disposed of. Dead bodies are an essential part of the natural food chain. Feeding flesh to fires is a waste."

"Why did they stop using the stream?" I asked.

"Bodies got stuck," Seba cackled. "They piled up a short way down the tunnel. The stench was unbearable. A team of vampires had to tie ropes around themselves and swim down the tunnel to hack the bodies free. They were pulled back by their colleagues, since nobody could swim against so furious a current.

"I was on that work detail," Seba continued. "Thankfully I only had to pull on the rope and did not have to venture into the water. Those who went down the tunnel to free the bodies could never bring themselves to talk of what they found."

As I gazed down at the dark water of the stream, shivering at the idea of swimming down the tunnel to pry loose stuck corpses, a thought struck me, and I turned to Kurda. "You say the bodies washed up for animals and birds to feed on — but isn't vampire blood poisonous?"

"There wasn't any blood," Kurda said.

"Why not?" I frowned.

Kurda hesitated, and Seba answered for him. "It had been drained by the Guardians of the Blood, who also removed most of their internal organs."

"Who are the Guardians of the Blood?" I asked.

"Do you remember the people we saw in the Hall of Cremation and the Hall of Death when I took you on a tour of the mountain?" Kurda said.

I cast my mind back and recalled the strange, ultrapale people with the eerie white eyes, dressed in rags, sitting alone and quiet in the somber Halls. Kurda had been reluctant to discuss them and said he'd tell me about them later, but with all that had happened since, I'd forgotten to follow up on the mystery. "Who are they?" I asked. "What do they do?"

"They're the Guardians of the Blood," Kurda said. "They came to Vampire Mountain more than a thousand years ago — we don't know from where — and have lived here ever since, though small bands go off wandering every decade or so, sometimes returning with new members. They have separate living quarters beneath the Halls and rarely mix with us. They also have their own language, customs, and beliefs."

"Are they humans?" I asked.

"They're ghouls!" Gavner grunted.

"That is unfair," Seba tutted. "They are loyal servants, deserving of our gratitude. They are in charge of the cremation ceremonies and do a noble job of preparing the dead. Plus, they provide us with blood — that is where most of the human blood in our stores comes from. We could never ship in enough to supply the needs of all the vampires at Council, so we rely upon the Guardians. They do not let us feed directly from them, but they extract their blood themselves and pass it to us in jars."

"Why?" I asked, perplexed. "It can't be much fun, living inside a mountain and giving their blood away. What's in it for them?"

Kurda coughed uncomfortably. "Do you know what a saprotroph is?"

I shook my head.

"They're creatures — or small organisms — which

feed on the waste or dead bodies of others. The Guardians are saprotrophs. They eat the internal organs — including the hearts and brains — of dead vampires."

I stared at Kurda, wondering if he was joking. But I saw by his grim expression that he wasn't. "Why do you let them?" I cried, my insides churning.

"We need them," Seba said plainly. "Their blood is necessary. Besides, they do us no harm."

"You don't think eating dead bodies is harmful?" I gasped.

"We haven't had any complaints from the dead yet," Gavner chortled, but his humor was forced — he looked as uncomfortable as I felt.

"They take great care with the bodies," Seba explained. "We are sacred to them. They drain the blood off first and store it in special casks of their own making — that is how they got their name — then delicately cut the torso open and remove the required organs. They also extract the brain, by inserting small hooks up the corpse's nose and pulling it out in little pieces."

"*What?*" Gavner roared. "I've never heard that before!"

"Most vampires are not aware of it," Seba said.

"But I have studied the Guardians in some detail over the centuries. The skulls of vampires are precious to them, and they never slice them apart."

"That's somewhat unsettling," Kurda murmured distastefully.

"It's disgraceful!" Gavner snorted.

"Cool!" I said.

"Once the organs and brains have been removed," Seba continued, "they cook them to make them safe — our blood is as deadly to the Guardians as it is to any creature."

"And that's what they live on?" I asked, revolted but fascinated.

"No," Seba replied. "They would not survive very long if that was their only intake. They eat normal food, preserving and reserving our organs for special occasions — they eat them at marriages, funerals, and other such events."

"That's disgusting!" I shouted, torn between ghoulish laughter and moral outrage. "Why do they do it?"

"We're not sure what the appeal is," Kurda admitted, "but part of it may be that it keeps them alive longer. The average Guardian lives a hundred and sixty years or more. Of course, if they became vampires, they'd live even longer, but none do — accepting a

CHAPTER TEN

vampire's blood is taboo as far as the Guardians are concerned."

"How can you let them do it?" I asked. "Why not send these monsters away?"

"They are not monsters," Seba disagreed. "They are people with peculiar feeding habits — much like ourselves! Besides, we drink their blood. It is a fair arrangement — our organs for their blood."

"*Fair* isn't the word I'd use," I muttered. "It's cannibalism!"

"Not really," Kurda objected. "They don't eat the flesh of their own, so they're not really cannibals."

"You're nitpicking," I grunted.

"It is a thin line," Seba agreed, "but there *is* a difference. I would not want to be a Guardian, and I do not socialize with them, but they are just odd humans getting along as best they can. Do not forget that *we* feed off people too, Darren. It would be wrong to despise them, just as it is wrong for humans to hate vampires."

"I told you this would turn morbid." Gavner chuckled.

"You were right." Kurda smiled. "This is a realm of the dead, not the living, and we should leave them to it. Let's get back to the Festival."

"Have you seen enough, Darren?" Seba asked.

"Yes." I shivered. "And I heard enough too!"

"Then let us depart."

We set off, Seba in front, Gavner and Kurda fast on his heels. I hung back a moment, studying the stream, listening to the roar of the water as it entered and exited the cave, thinking about the Guardians of the Blood, imagining my dead, drained, hollowed body making the long descent down the mountain, tossed like a rag doll from rock to rock.

It was a horrible image. Shaking my head, I thrust it from my thoughts and hurried after my friends, unaware that within a frighteningly short time I would be back at this same gruesome spot, not to mourn the passing of somebody else's life — but to fight desperately for my own!

CHAPTER ELEVEN

THE FESTIVAL of the Undead came to a grand, elaborate close on the third night. The celebrations started several hours before sunset, and though the Festival officially ended with the coming of night, a number of vampires kept the party spirit alive late into the following morning.

There was no fighting during the final day of the Festival. The time was given over to storytelling, music, and singing. I learned much about our history and ancestors — the names of great vampire leaders, fierce battles we'd fought with humans and vampaneze — and would have stayed to listen right through the night if I had not had to leave to learn about my next Trial.

This time I picked the Hall of Flames, and every

vampire in attendance looked grim-faced when the Trial was called out.

"It's bad, isn't it?" I asked Vanez.

"Yes," the games master answered truthfully. "It will be your hardest Trial yet. We will ask Arra to help us prepare. With her help, you might pull through."

He stressed the word *might*.

I spent most of the following day and night learning to dodge fire. The Hall of Flames was a large metal room with lots of holes in the floor. Fierce fires would be lit outside the Hall when it was time for the Trial, and vampires would use bellows to pump flames into the room and up through the floor. Because there were so many pipes leading from the fires to the holes, it was impossible to predict the path the flames would follow and where they would emerge.

"You must use your ears as much as your eyes," Arra instructed. The vampiress had injured her right arm during the Festival, and it was in a sling. "You can hear the flames coming before you see them."

One of the fires had been lit outside the Hall, and a couple of vampires pumped flames from it into the room so that I could learn to recognize the sound of the fire traveling through the pipes. Arra stood behind me, pushing me out of the way of the flames if I failed to react quickly enough. "You hear the hissing?" she asked.

"Yes."

"That is the sound of flames passing by you. It's when you hear a short whistling sound — like that!" she snapped, tugging me back as a pillar of fire sprouted from the floor at my feet. "Did you hear it?"

"Just about," I said, trembling nervously.

"That's not good enough." She frowned. "*Just about* will kill you. You have very little time to beat the flames. Every fraction of a second is precious. It's no good to re-act immediately — you must react *in advance.*"

A few hours later, I had the hang of it and was darting around the Hall, avoiding the flames with ease. "That's good," Arra said as we rested. "But only one fire burns at the moment. Come the time of your Trial, all five will be lit. The flames will come quicker and in greater volume. You have much to learn before you are ready."

After more practice, Arra took me outside the Hall and over to the fire. She shoved me up close to it, grabbed a burning branch, and ran it over the flesh of my legs and arms. "Stop!" I screeched. "You're burning me alive!"

"Be still!" she commanded. "You must accustom yourself to the heat. Your skin is tough — you can stand a lot of punishment. But you must be ready for it. Nobody makes it through the Hall of Flames unmarked. You *will* be burnt and singed. Your chances of emerging alive depend on how you react to your injuries. If you let yourself feel the pain, and panic — you'll die. If not, you might survive."

I knew she wouldn't say these things unless they were true, so I stood still and ground my teeth together while she ran the glowing tip of the branch over my flesh. The itching, which had all but disappeared following Seba's application of the cobwebs, flared into life again, adding to my misery.

During a break, I studied my flesh where Arra had run the flaming branch over it. It was a nasty pink color and stung when touched, like a bad case of sunburn. "Are you sure this is a good idea?" I asked.

"You must grow used to the lick of flames," Arra said. "The more pain we subject your body to now, the easier it will be to cope later. Be under no illusions — this is one of the most difficult Trials. You will suffer before the end."

"You're not exactly filling me with confidence," I moaned.

"I'm not here to fill you with confidence," she replied. "I'm here to help you save your life."

After a short discussion between Vanez and Arra, it was decided that I should go without my usual few hours of sleep before the Trial. "We need those extra hours," Vanez said. "You've had three days and nights of rest. Right now, practice is more important than sleep."

So, after a brief break, it was back to the Hall and the fire, where I learned how to *narrowly* dodge flames. It was best to move around as little as possible during the Trial. That way you could listen more intently and concentrate on predicting where the next burst of flames was coming from. It meant getting singed and lightly burnt, but that was preferable to taking a wrong step and going up in a cloud of smoke.

We practiced until half an hour before the start of the Trial. I nipped back to my cell to catch my breath and change clothes — I'd be wearing leather shorts, nothing else — then returned to the Hall of Flames, where many vampires had gathered to wish me well.

Arrow — the bald-headed, tattooed Prince — had come from the Hall of Princes to oversee the Trial. "I'm sorry none of us could make it last time," he apologized, making the death's touch sign.

"That's OK," I told him. "I don't mind."

"You are a gracious competitor," Arrow said. "Now, do you know the rules?"

I nodded. "I have to stay in there fifteen minutes and try not to get roasted."

"Well put." The Prince grinned. "Are you ready?"

"Almost," I said, knees knocking together. I turned to face Mr. Crepsley. "If I don't pull through, I want you to —", I began, but he interrupted angrily.

"Do not talk like that! Think positively."

"I am thinking positively," I said, "but I know how difficult it will be. All I was going to say was, I've been thinking it over, and if I die, I'd like you to take my body home and bury it in my grave. That way I'll be close to Mom, Dad, and Annie."

Mr. Crepsley's eyes twitched (was he blinking back *tears?*) and he cleared his throat. "I will do as you request," he croaked, then offered me his hand. I brushed it aside and gave him a hug instead.

"I'm proud to have been your assistant," I whispered in his ear, then pulled away before he could say anything else and entered the Hall of Flames.

The door clanging shut behind me cut off the sound of the fires being stoked up. I walked towards the center of the room, sweating freely from the heat and fear. The floor was already hot. I wanted to rub some spit on my feet, to cool them, but Arra had told me not to do that too soon. Things would get a whole lot hotter later — better to hold some spit back for when I really needed it.

There was a gurgling sound from the pipes below. I tensed, but it was only one of the pipes shaking. Relaxing, I closed my eyes and swallowed deep breaths while there was still clean air to breathe. That was another problem I'd have to face — although there were holes in the roof and walls, oxygen would be in short supply, and I'd have to find air pockets among the flames or risk suffocating.

As I was thinking about the air, I heard an angry hissing sound in the floor beneath me. Opening my eyes, I saw a jagged funnel of flame erupt several feet to my left.

The Trial had begun.

I ignored the spouting flames — they were too far away to harm me — and listened closely for the next burst. This time it came from one of the far corners of the room. I was off to a lucky start. Sometimes, according to Arra, flames struck at you right at the beginning and didn't let up for the entire Trial. At least I had time to adjust to the heat gradually.

There was a whistling sound close to my right. I jumped aside as fire blossomed in the air nearby, then scolded myself — that burst had been close, but it wouldn't have struck. I should have stood my ground or edged carefully out of its way. Moving as I had, I could have stepped straight into trouble.

The flames were coming in quick bursts now, all around the Hall. I could feel a terrible heat building in the air, and already it was hard to breathe. A hole a few inches from my right foot whistled. I didn't move as fire erupted and stung my leg — I could tolerate a small burn like that. A large burst came out of a wider hole behind me. I shifted forward slightly, rolling gently away from the worst of its bite. I felt the flames licking at the skin of my bare back, but none took hold.

The hardest times were when two or more funnels sprang from holes set close together. There was nothing I could do when trapped between a set of fiery pillars, except suck in my belly and step gingerly through the thinner wall of flames.

Within a few minutes my feet were in agony — they absorbed the worst of the flames. I spat on my palms and rubbed spit into my soles, which provided some measure of temporary relief. I would have stood on my hands to give my feet a rest, except that would have exposed my hair to the fire.

Most vampires, when preparing for the Trials, shaved their heads months in advance, so they were bald when the Trials began. That way, if they drew the Hall of Flames, they'd stand a better chance, since hair burns a lot easier than flesh. But you weren't allowed to shave your head *especially* for the Trial, and things had happened so quickly with me that nobody had thought to prepare me for the possibility of facing the flames.

There was no way to keep track of time. I had to focus every last ounce of my concentration on the floor and fire. The smallest of distractions could have lethal consequences.

Several holes in front of me spouted flames at the same time. I began edging backwards, when I heard pipes whistling savagely behind me. Sucking in my belly again, I nudged over to my left, away from the thickest sheets of fire.

The moment of danger passed, but I was getting trapped in a corner. Vanez had warned me about this, even before we'd tracked down Arra and asked her to train me. "Stay away from the corners," he'd said. "Stick to the middle as much as possible. If you find yourself backing into a corner, get out of it quickly. Most who perish in the Hall of Flames do so in corners, trapped by walls of fire, unable to break free."

I started back the way I'd come, but the fire was still shooting up through the holes, blocking my path. Reluctantly, I edged farther towards the corner, ready to take the first opening as soon as one presented itself. The trouble was — none did.

The gurgling of pipes behind me brought me to a halt. Flames burst out of the floor, scorching my back. I grimaced but didn't move — there was nowhere to move to. The air was very poor in this region of the room. I waved my hands in front of my face, trying to create a draft to suck some fresh air in, but it didn't work.

The pillars of flames in front of me had formed a wall of fire, at least seven or eight feet thick. I could barely see the rest of the room through the flickering flames. As I stood, waiting for a path to open, the mouths of the pipes at my feet hissed, several of them all at once. A huge ball of fire was on its way, about to explode directly underneath me! I had a split second to think and act.

Couldn't stand still — I'd burn.

Couldn't retreat — I'd burn.

Couldn't duck to the sides — I'd burn.

CHAPTER ELEVEN

Forward, through the thick banks of fire? I'd probably burn, but there was open ground and air beyond — *if* I made it through. It was a lousy choice, but there was no time to complain. Closing my eyes and mouth, I covered my face with my arms and darted forward into the wall of crackling flames.

CHAPTER TWELVE

Fire engulfed and billowed around me. I'd never in my worst nightmare imagined such heat. I almost opened my mouth to scream. If I had, fire would have gushed down my throat and torched me to a crisp from the inside out.

When I burst through the other side of the fiery wall, my hair was a burning bush, and flames sprouted from my body like mushrooms. I dropped to the floor and rolled around, beating at my hair with my hands, extinguishing the flames. I paid no attention to the hisses and whistlings of the pipes. If flames had struck in those seconds of madness, they'd have devoured me. But I got lucky . . . lucky Darren Shan . . . the luck of the vampires.

Once I'd slapped out the worst of the flames, I got to my knees, groaning weakly. Sucking in hot, thin air,

I prodded gently at the smoldering mess on top of my head, making sure there were no sparks waiting to flare back to life.

My entire body was black and red. Black from the soot, red where the burns had eaten through my flesh. I was in bad shape, but I had to go on. Sore as I was, and painful as it was to move, I had to. The ravenous demons of the fire would devour me if I didn't.

Standing, I tuned out the roars of the flames and listened for the sounds of the pipes. It wasn't easy — my ears had been savagely burnt, affecting my sense of hearing — but I was able to detect the faintest hints of hissing and whistling, and after a few shaky steps I was back on course, anticipating the bursts of flames and moving to avoid them.

The one good thing about wading through the wall of fire was that it had burnt out much of the feelings in my feet. There was almost no pain now beneath my knees. That meant I was dangerously singed, and part of me worried about what would happen after the Trial — if my feet were burnt beyond repair, they might have to be amputated! — but that was a worry for another time. Right now I was glad for the relief and took comfort from it.

My ears were seriously troubling me. I tried to rub some spit on them, but my mouth had dried up completely. I caressed them gently between my fingers, but that made them worse. In the end I left them alone and just did my best to ignore them.

The flames were forcing me into another corner. Rather than let myself get trapped again, I ducked through a roaring bank of fire and back to open ground, enduring the ensuing pain.

I closed my eyes as often as possible, every time there was the slightest lull. The heat was dreadful for them. They'd dried up the same way my mouth had, and I was afraid of losing my sight.

As I rolled away from yet another nasty burst of fire, the flames in the Hall began to die away. I paused suspiciously. Was this the start of an even worse assault? Could I expect a huge ball of fire to burst through the pipes and blow me away?

While I twitched and strained my ears, the door to the Hall swung open, and vampires in heavy capes entered. I stared at them as though they were aliens. What were they doing? Were they firemen who'd lost their way? Someone should tell them they shouldn't be here. It was dangerous.

I backed away from the vampires as they converged on me. I'd have warned them to get out before the next big ball of fire hit, except I had no voice. I couldn't even manage a squeak. "Darren, it is over," one of the vampires said. He sounded like Mr. Crepsley, but it couldn't be — Mr. Crepsley wouldn't wander into a Hall during the middle of a Trial.

I waved a singed hand at the vampires and mouthed the words, "Go away! Get out of here!"

"Darren," the lead vampire said again, "it is over. You won!"

I couldn't make sense of his words. All I knew was that a huge ball of fire was due, and if these fools were blocking my way, I'd be incapable of dodging it. Hitting out at them, I tried weaving my way through their arms to safety. I ducked the grasp of the lead vampire, but the next caught me by the scruff of the neck. His touch was painful and I dropped to the floor, screaming silently.

"Be careful!" the lead vampire snapped, then bent over me — it *was* Mr. Crepsley! "Darren," he said softly, "it is all right. You did it. You are safe."

Shaking my head, unable to think clearly, I mouthed the same word over and over: "Fire! Fire! Fire!"

I was still mouthing it when they lifted me onto a stretcher and carted me from the Hall. And even when we were outside, clear of the flames, and medics were tending to my wounds, I couldn't stop my lips from forming the word of warning, or my eyes from rolling to the left and right, fearfully searching for the telltale signs of red and yellow terror.

CHAPTER THIRTEEN

MY CELL. Lying on my belly. Medics examining my back, rubbing cool lotions into my skin. Somebody lifting my charred feet, gasping, calling for help.

Gazing at the ceiling. Someone holding a torch up to my eyes, peering into my pupils. A razor running over my head, scalping me, removing the remains of my burnt hair. Gavner Purl stepping forward, worried. "I think he's —" he starts to say. Darkness.

Nightmares. The world on fire. Running. Burning. Screaming. Calling for help. Everybody else on fire too.

Jolt awake. Vampires around me. Nightmare still playing at the back of my mind. Convinced the cell's on fire. I try to break free. They hold me down. I curse them. Struggle. Pain gushes through me. Wince. Relax. Return to fire-plagued dreams.

Finally I drifted back from the lands of delirium. I was lying facedown. I moved my head slightly to gaze around the cell. Mr. Crepsley and Harkat Mulds were sitting nearby, monitoring me.

"Thought . . . I saw . . . Gavner," I wheezed.

Mr. Crepsley and Harkat sprang forward, smiling worriedly. "He was here earlier," Mr. Crepsley said. "So were Kurda, Vanez, and Arra. The medics told them to leave."

"I . . . made it?" I asked.

"Yes."

"How bad . . . am I . . . burnt?"

"Very bad," Mr. Crepsley said.

"You look . . . like an over- . . . cooked sausage," Harkat joked.

I laughed weakly. "I sound . . . like you . . . now," I told him.

"Yes," he agreed. "But you . . . will get . . . better."

"Will I?" I addressed the question to Mr. Crepsley.

"Yes," he said, nodding firmly. "You have suffered a terrible ordeal, but the damage is not permanent. Your feet suffered the worst of the punishment, but the medics have saved them. It will take time to heal, and your hair might never grow back, but you are in no immediate danger."

"I feel . . . terrible," I told him.

"Be glad you can feel at all," he replied bluntly.

"What about . . . next Trial?"

"Do not think of such things now."

"I . . . must," I gasped. "Will I . . . have time . . . to get ready . . . for it?"

Mr. Crepsley didn't say anything.

"Tell me . . . the truth," I insisted.

"There will be no extra time," he sighed. "Kurda is in the Hall of Princes as we speak, arguing your case, but he will not be able to persuade them to postpone. There is no precedent for a delay between Trials. Those unfit to continue must . . ." He came to a stop.

". . . be taken to . . . the Hall of . . . Death," I finished for him.

While he sat there, trying to think of something comforting to say, Kurda returned, looking flushed with excitement. "Is he awake?" he asked.

"I am," I answered.

Crouching beside me, he said, "It's almost sunset. You must choose your next Trial or admit failure and be carted away for execution. If we carry you to the Hall of Princes, do you think you'll be able to stand upright for a couple of minutes?"

"I'm not . . . sure," I answered honestly. "My feet . . . hurt."

"I know," he said. "But it's important. I've found a way to buy us some time, but only if you can act as if you're fine."

"What *way?*" Mr. Crepsley asked, astonished.

"No time for explanations," Kurda snapped. "Are you willing to give it a try, Darren?"

I nodded weakly.

"Good. Let's get him on a stretcher and up to the Hall of Princes. We can't be late."

Hurrying through the tunnels, we made it to the Hall just in time for sunset. Vanez Blane was outside, waiting with his purple flag. "What's going on, Kurda?" he asked. "There's no way Darren will be ready to face a Trial tomorrow."

"Trust me," Kurda said. "It was Paris's idea, but we can't let on. We have to act as if we're ready to continue. It all hinges on Darren standing up and drawing his Trial. Come on. And remember — we *have to* act like there's nothing wrong."

We were all mystified by Kurda's behavior, but we had no choice except to do what he said. Entering the Hall of Princes, I heard the voices of the vampires within drop, as all eyes fixed upon us. Kurda and Mr. Crepsley carried me to the platform of the Princes, Harkat and Vanez just behind.

"Is this young Master Shan?" Paris asked.

"It is, sire," Kurda answered.

"He looks terrible," Mika Ver Leth noted. "Are you sure he's fit to continue with the Trials?"

"He is merely resting, sire," Kurda said lightly. "He likes to pretend to be injured, so that he can be carried around like a lord."

"Really?" Mika replied, smiling tightly. "If that is the case, let the boy step forward and choose his next Trial. You understand," he added ominously, "what we must do if he is unable?"

"We understand," Kurda said as he laid his end of the stretcher down. Mr. Crepsley followed suit. The two vampires helped me to my feet, then slowly let go of me. I teetered dangerously and almost fell. I probably would have, if there hadn't been so many vampires present — but I didn't want to look frail in front of them.

Fighting the pain, I stumbled forward to the platform. It took a long time to make it up the steps, but I didn't falter. Nobody said anything while I was climbing, and when I got there the bag of numbered stones was produced and checked as normal. "Number four," the vampire clutching the bag announced once I'd drawn my stone. "The Blooded Boars."

"A tricky Trial," Paris Skyle mused as the stone was passed to the Princes to be certified. "Are you ready for it, Darren?"

"I don't . . . know what it . . . is," I said. "But . . . I will be . . . there to face it . . . tomorrow, as . . . scheduled."

Paris smiled warmly. "That is good to hear." He cleared his throat and widened his eyes innocently. "*I*, however, cannot make it. I have pressing business to attend to and regretfully must miss this Trial. My good colleague Mika will take my place."

Mika imitated Paris's innocent look. "Actually, I can't get away from the Hall tomorrow either. This Vampaneze Lord business takes up all my time. How about you, Arrow?"

The bald Prince shook his head glumly. "Alas, *I* also must make my excuses. My schedule is full."

"Sires," Kurda said, quickly stepping forward. "You have already skipped one of Darren's Trials. We allowed for your absence on that occasion, but to neglect your post twice in the course of one set of Trials is unpardonable and does Darren a grave disservice. I must protest most strongly."

Paris started to smile, caught himself, and forced a scowl. "There is truth in your words," he muttered.

"We cannot miss another of the boy's Trials," Mika agreed.

"One way or another, one of us must be present," Arrow finished.

The three Princes huddled close together and discussed it quietly. By the way they smirked and winked at Kurda, I knew they had something up their sleeves.

"Very well," Paris said out loud. "Darren has reported that he is fit for his next Trial. Since we cannot be there to oversee it, we have decided to postpone it. We apologize for the inconvenience, Darren. Will you pardon us?"

"I'll let . . . it pass . . . this time." I grinned.

"How long must we wait, sires?" Kurda asked, acting impatient. "Darren is anxious to finish his Trials."

"Not long," Paris said. "One of us will be there for the Trial at sunset, seventy-two hours from now. Is that agreeable?"

"It is annoying, sire," — Kurda sighed theatrically — "but if we have to wait, we will."

Bowing, Kurda led me from the platform, helped me back onto the stretcher, and carried me from the

Hall with Mr. Crepsley. Once outside, the vampires set me down and laughed loudly.

"You scoundrel, Kurda Smahlt!" Mr. Crepsley roared. "How did you dream that one up?"

"It was Paris's idea," Kurda replied humbly. "The Princes wanted to help Darren, but they couldn't turn around and say they were giving him time to recover from his injuries. They needed an excuse to save face. This way, it looks as though Darren was ready and willing to proceed, so there's no shame in postponing it."

"That's why . . . I had to stand," I noted. "So nobody would be . . . suspicious."

"Correct." Kurda beamed. "Everyone in the Hall knows what's really happening, but as long as it *looks* as if everything is in order, nobody will object."

"Three nights . . . and days," I mused. "Will it be . . . enough?"

"If not, it will not be for want of trying," Mr. Crepsley said with fierce determination, and we set off down the tunnels at a brisk pace to find some medics capable of knocking me back into shape before I had to face the Blooded Boars.

CHAPTER FOURTEEN

TIME PASSED slowly while I was confined to my recovery hammock. Medics fussed over me, rubbing lotions into my charred flesh, changing bandages, cleaning the wounds, making sure infection didn't set in. They often commented on how fortunate I was. None of the damage was permanent, except maybe the hair loss. My feet would heal, my lungs were OK, most of my skin would grow back. All things considered, I was in great shape and should thank my lucky stars.

But I didn't *feel* like I was in great shape. I was in pain the whole time. It was bad enough when I lay still but grew unbearable when I moved. I cried into my pillow a lot, wishing I could fall asleep and not wake until the pain had passed, but even in sleep I was tortured by the aftereffects of the fire, terrorized by nightmares, never more than a sharp twinge away from wakefulness.

I had plenty of visitors, who helped distract me from the pain. Seba and Gavner spent hours by my side, telling me stories and jokes. Gavner had started calling me Toastie, because he said I looked like a slice of burnt toast. And he offered to find a charred torch stub and draw fake ashen eyebrows on my forehead, since my own had been burnt off along with my head of hair. I told him where he could stick his torch stub — and the rest of the torch as well!

I asked Seba if he had any special cures for burns, hoping the old vampire would know of some traditional remedy that the medics were ignorant of. "Alas, no," he said, "but when your wounds have healed, we shall make another trip to the caves of Ba'Halen's spiders and find cobwebs to prevent further itching."

Arra often came to see me, though she spent more time talking with Mr. Crepsley than to me. The two spent a lot of time talking about the old nights and their life together when they were mates.

After a while I fell to wondering if the pair might be planning to mate again and how that would affect my relationship with the vampire. When I asked Mr. Crepsley about it, he coughed with embarrassment and snapped that I shouldn't bother him with such nonsense — Arra and he were just good friends.

"*Of course* you are." I chuckled, giving him a knowing wink.

Kurda could only get down to see me a couple of times. Now that the Festival of the Undead was out of the way, there was a lot of business for the vampires to discuss, much of it connected to the vampaneze. As a senior General and vampaneze expert, he had to spend most of his waking hours in meetings and conferences.

Arra was with me on one of the rare occasions when Kurda came. She stiffened when she saw him, and he started to withdraw, to avoid a confrontation. "Wait," she called him back. "I want to thank you for what you did for Darren."

"It was nothing." He smiled.

"It wasn't," she disagreed. "Many of us care about Darren, but only you had sense enough to steer him to safety in his hour of need. The rest of us would have stood by and watched him die. I don't agree with your ways — there's a thin line between diplomacy and cowardice — but sometimes they *do* work better than our own."

Arra left, and Kurda smiled lightly. "Do you know," he remarked, "that's the closest she'll ever get to saying she likes me."

Kurda fed me some water — I was on a liquids-only diet — and told me what had been happening while I was out of action. A committee had been established to discuss the workings of the vampaneze and what to do in the event of the emergence of a Vampaneze Lord. "For the first time, they're seriously talking about making peace with the vampaneze," he said.

"That must make you happy."

He sighed. "If this had happened a few years ago, I'd have been whooping with glee. But time's running out. I think it's going to take more than a mere committee to unite the tribes and combat the threat of the Vampaneze Lord."

"I thought you didn't believe in the Vampaneze Lord," I said.

He shrugged. "Officially, I don't. Between you and me . . ." — He lowered his voice — "The thought of him scares me silly."

"You think he's real?" I asked.

"If Mr. Tiny says so — yes. Whatever else I believe or don't believe in, there's no doubting the powers of Mr. Tiny. Unless we act quickly to prevent the possibility of a Vampaneze Lord arising, I'm sure he'll come. Stopping him before he gets started may involve a terrible sacrifice, but if that's the price of averting a war, so be it."

It was odd to hear Kurda making such a confession. If he — friend to the vampaneze — was worried, the other vampires must be terrified. I hadn't been paying a lot of attention to talk of the Vampaneze Lord, but I made up my mind to listen more closely in the future.

The next night — the last before the start of my fourth Trial — Mr. Crepsley came to see me after a meeting with Vanez Blane. Harkat was already by my hammock. The Little Person had spent more time with me than anyone else.

"I have discussed things with Vanez," Mr. Crepsley said, "and we both agree that you would be better served in preparing for your next Trial by rest rather than practice. There are no special skills required in the Trial of the Blooded Boars. You simply have to face and kill two boars that have been infected with vampire blood. It is a straightforward fight to the death."

"If I can beat a wild bear, I can beat a couple of boars." I grinned, trying to sound upbeat — I'd killed a savage bear during our trek to Vampire Mountain.

"Most certainly you can," Mr. Crepsley agreed. "Were it not for your wounds, I would even hazard a guess that you could do it with one arm tied behind your back."

I smiled, then coughed. I'd been coughing a lot

since the Hall of Flames. It was a natural reaction to all the smoke I'd inhaled. My lungs hadn't suffered any serious damage, so the coughing should stop in another couple of days. Mr. Crepsley handed me a glass of water, and I sipped from it slowly. I was able to feed myself now and had enjoyed my first meal since the Hall of Flames earlier in the night. I was still in pretty bad shape, but thanks to my vampire blood, I was recovering quickly.

"Do you feel ready for the Trial?" Mr. Crepsley asked.

"I'd like another twenty-four hours," I sighed, "but I think I'll be OK. I walked around for fifteen minutes after breakfast and I felt good. As long as my legs and feet hold, I should be fine — fingers crossed."

"I have been talking to Seba Nile," Mr. Crepsley said, switching subjects. "He tells me he is thinking of retiring once Council has ended. He feels he has served long enough as the quartermaster of Vampire Mountain. He wants to see the world one last time before he dies."

"Maybe he can come with us to the Cirque Du Freak," I suggested.

"Actually," Mr. Crepsley said, watching closely for my reaction, "we might not be returning to the Cirque Du Freak."

"Oh?" I frowned.

"Seba has offered me the job of quartermaster. I am thinking of accepting it."

"I thought nobody liked becoming quartermaster," I said.

"It is not much sought after," Mr. Crepsley agreed, "but quartermasters are widely respected. The running of Vampire Mountain is a great responsibility. It can also be richly rewarding — for hundreds of years you arc capable of influencing the lives of every new Vampire General."

"Why did he offer the job to you?" I asked. "Why not one of his assistants?"

"His assistants are young. They dream of being Generals or going out into the world and making a mark of their own. It would be unfair to tear one of them away from his dreams when I am at hand, ready and able to step into the position."

"You want to do this, don't you?" I asked, reading his desire in his expression.

He nodded. "A decade or two ago, it would have been the furthest thing from my wishes. But life has been aimless since I quit the Generals. I had not realized how much I missed being part of the clan until I attended this Council. This would be the ideal way for me to reestablish myself."

"If you want it that much, go for it," I encouraged him.

"But what about you?" he asked. "As my assistant, you would have to remain here with me until you are old enough to leave by yourself. Do you like the idea of spending the next thirty years of your life walled up inside this mountain?"

"Not really," I said. "I've enjoyed my stay — apart from the Trials — but I imagine it could grow boring after a couple of years." I ran a hand over my bald head and thought at length about it. "And there's Harkat to consider. How will he get back if we stay here?"

"I will . . . stay with you . . . if you decide . . . to remain," he said.

"You will?" I asked, surprised.

"Part of . . . my memory . . . has come back. Much is . . . still blank, but I . . . recall Mr. Tiny . . . telling me the only . . . way I could . . . find out who I . . . was before I died . . . was by . . . sticking with you."

"How can I help you find out who you were?" I asked.

Harkat shrugged. "I do not . . . know. But I will . . . stay by your . . . side, as long . . . as you will . . . have me."

"You don't mind being cooped up inside a mountain?" I asked.

Harkat smiled. "Little People . . . are easily . . . pleased."

I lay back and considered the proposal. If I stayed, I could learn more about the ways of the vampires, perhaps even train to be a Vampire General. The idea of being a General appealed to me — I could picture myself leading a troop of vampires into battle with the vampaneze, like a pirate captain or an officer in the army.

On the other hand, I'd maybe never see Evra Von or Mr. Tall or my other friends at the Cirque Du Freak again. No more traveling around the world, performing for audiences, or luxury comforts like going to the movies or ordering Chinese take-out — not for thirty-odd years at least!

"It's a huge decision," I mused aloud. "Can I have some time to think it over?"

"Of course," Mr. Crepsley said. "There is no rush. Seba expects no answer until after Council. We will discuss it in further detail when you have concluded your Trials."

"*If* I conclude them." I grinned nervously.

"*When*," Mr. Crepsley insisted, and smiled reassuringly.

CHAPTER FIFTEEN

THE FOURTH Trial — the Blooded Boars.

It seemed as if half the vampires in the mountain had turned out to watch me take on the two wild boars. I learned, as I waited for the Trial to start, that interest in me was at an all-time high. Many vampires had expected me to fail long before this. They were amazed that I'd survived the Hall of Flames. Already the storytellers of Vampire Mountain were busy turning my exploits into the stuff of modern legend. I heard one of them describing my Trial on the Path of Needles, and to listen to him tell it, I'd endured ten avalanches and been pierced clean through the stomach by a falling stalactite, which had to be cut out of me after the Trial!

It was fun listening to the murmured stories

spreading through the crowds of vampires, even if most was nonsense. They made me feel like King Arthur or Alexander the Great.

"Don't go getting a swelled head," Gavner laughed, noting the way I was listening intently to the tales. He was keeping me company while Vanez chose my weapons. "Exaggeration is the key to every legend. If you fail in this or the final Trial, they'll make out that you were a lazy, stupid, good-for-nothing and hold you up as an example for future vampires. 'Work hard, my boy,' they'll say, 'or you'll end up like that wastrel Darren Shan.'"

"At least they won't be able to say I snored like a bear," I retorted.

Gavner grimaced. "You've been spending too much time around Larten," he growled.

Vanez returned and handed me a small spiked wooden club and a short spear. "These are the best I could do," he said, scratching the skin beneath his missing left eye with the tip of the spear. "They aren't much, but they'll have to do."

"These will be fine," I said, though I'd been hoping for something more deadly.

"You know what will happen?" he asked.

"The boars will be released into the ring at the same time. They might scrap with each other at the start, but as soon as they smell me, they'll focus on me."

Vanez nodded. "That's how the bear tracked you down on your way here, and why he attacked you. Vampiric blood heightens an animal's senses, especially its sense of smell. They go for whatever smells the strongest.

"You'll have to get close to the boars to kill them. Use your spear to stab at their eyes. Save your club for their snouts and skulls. Don't bother with their bodies — you'd be wasting your energy.

"The boars probably won't coordinate their attacks. Usually, when one moves in for the kill, the other hangs back. If they *do* come at you together, they might get in each other's way. Use their confusion if you can.

"Avoid their tusks. If you get stuck on a set, get off them quickly, even if you have to drop your weapons to free yourself. There's only so much damage they can do if you steer clear of their tusks."

A bugle call announced the arrival of Mika Ver Leth, who would be presiding over the Trial. The black-garbed Prince bade me good evening and asked if I was ready to begin. I told him I was. He wished me luck and made the death's touch sign, checked to make sure I was carrying no concealed weapons, then swept away to take his position, while I was led into the arena.

The arena was a big round pit in the ground. A sturdy wooden fence had been built around it to make sure the boars couldn't escape. Vampires stood around the fence, cheering like a crowd of Romans at the Colosseum.

I stretched my arms above my head and winced at the pain. Much of my flesh was tender, and some of my wounds were already seeping beneath my bandages. My feet weren't too painful — a lot of the nerve endings had been burnt out, and it would be weeks, maybe months, before they grew back — but I stung piercingly everywhere else.

The doors to the pit swung open, and two caged boars were dragged in by guards. A hush settled over the observing vampires. Once the guards had retreated and shut the doors, the locks of the cages were undone by overhead wires, and the cages were lifted out of the pit by ropes. The boars grunted angrily when they found themselves in the open. They immediately head-butted each other, locking tusks. They were fierce creatures, five feet long, maybe three feet high.

When my scent reached the pair, they stopped fighting and backed away from each other. One spotted me and squealed. The other followed the gaze of the first, set its sights on me, and charged. I raised my spear defensively. The boar turned about ten feet away from where I was standing and wheeled off to one side, snorting savagely.

The far-off boar trotted towards me, slowly, purposefully. It stopped several feet away, eyed me evilly, pawed the ground with its hooves, then darted. I easily avoided its lunge and managed to strike one of its ears with the head of my club as it sped past. It roared, made a quick turn, and came at me again. I jumped over it this time, jabbing at its eyes with my spear, missing narrowly. When I landed, the second boar attacked. It threw itself at me, opening and shutting its jaws like a shark, twirling its tusks wildly.

I dodged the assault but stumbled as I did. Because of the destroyed nerve endings in my feet, I realized I couldn't rely on them as much as I used to. Numbness in my soles meant I could trip at any time, without warning. I'd have to tread carefully.

One of the boars saw me stumbling and rammed me hard from the side. Luckily, its tusks didn't catch, and though the blow knocked the wind out of me, I was able to roll away and regain my balance.

I didn't have much time to get ready for the next attack. Almost before I knew it, a huge hunk of heaving flesh was coming straight at me. Acting on instinct,

I stepped aside and thrust with my spear. There was a loud yelp, and when I raised the tip of the spear it was red with blood.

There was a brief respite while the boars circled me. It was easy to spot the one I'd injured — there was a long gash down one side of its snout, from which blood was dripping — but it wasn't a serious injury and would do little to prevent more attacks.

The bloodied boar half lunged at me. I waved my club at it, and it spun away, snorting. The other made a serious run, but lowered its head too soon, so I was able to avoid it by stepping quickly aside.

The vampires overhead were yelling advice and encouragement, but I drowned out the sound of their cries and focused on the boars. They were circling me again, raking up dust with their hooves, taking deep determined breaths.

The unharmed boar suddenly stopped circling and charged. I edged aside, but it kept its head up and followed me. Tensing the muscles in my legs, I jumped and tried braining it with my club. But I'd mistimed my jump, and instead of connecting with the boar, the boar connected with me.

Its head and shoulders knocked my legs out from under me, and I fell heavily to the floor. The boar turned quickly and was over me before I could get up, its hot breath clouding my face, its tusks flashing dangerously in the dim light of the pit.

I slapped at the boar with my club, but was in no position to make the blows count. It shrugged them off and poked at me with its tusks. I felt one tusk cut through the bandages around my belly and slice shallowly into the burnt flesh beneath. If I didn't get moving soon, the boar would do real damage.

Taking hold of the round ball at the end of the club, I jammed it into the boar's mouth, muffling its eager snuffles. The boar retreated, grunting angrily. I scrambled to my feet. As I did, the second boar slammed into me from behind. I went tumbling over the first boar, rolled head over heels like a ball, and collided with the fence.

As I sat up, dazed, I heard the sound of a boar running straight at me. With no time to get a fix on it, I dived blindly to my left. The boar missed me, and there was a ferocious clattering as it struck the fence at full speed with its head.

I'd dropped my spear, but had time to retrieve it while the boar tottered away, shaking its head, confused. I was hoping it would collapse, but after a few seconds it had recovered and looked as mean and purposeful as ever.

My club was still stuck in the mouth of the other

boar. There was no way to get it back, not unless it fell out.

Taking a firm grip on my spear, I decided I'd conceded enough ground to the boars. It was time to take the fight to them. Crouching low, holding my spear out in front of me, I advanced. The boars didn't know what to make of my behavior. They made a couple of halfhearted lunges at me, then fell back warily. They obviously hadn't been infected with a large quantity of vampire blood, or they'd have attacked continuously, madly, regardless of safety.

As I herded them towards the far side of the pit, I focused on the boar with the bloody snout. It seemed to be the less secure of the two and retreated more quickly. There was a hint of cowardice about it.

I faked an attack on the braver boar with the club in its mouth, waving my spear in the air, so it turned and fled. As the other relaxed slightly, I changed course and leapt on it. I grabbed the boar by the neck and held on as it roared and bucked. It dragged me almost all the way around the pit before it ran out of steam and came to a stop. While it tried to snag with its tusks, I dug at its eyes with my spear. I missed, cut its snout, sliced its ear, missed again — then struck true and gouged its right eye out.

The roaring when the boar lost its eye almost deafened me. It tossed its head about wilder than ever and scratched my belly and chest with its tusks, but not seriously. I held on firmly, ignoring the pain in my hands and arms as burn wounds were torn open and blood flowed freely.

The vampires above me were very excited and cries of "Kill it! Kill it!" filled the air. I felt sorry for the boar — it only attacked me because it had been provoked — but it was him or me. This was no time for mercy.

I edged in front of the boar — a dangerous move — and readied myself for a frontal attack. I kept to the right, so it couldn't see me, held my spear high above my head, and waited for the right moment to strike. After a few frenzied seconds, the boar caught sight of me through its left eye and paused uncertainly, presenting a steady target. Bringing my arm down sharply, I drove the tip of the spear through the gap where the right eye had been, deep into the boar's crazed brain.

There was a horrible squishing sound, then the boar went mad. Rearing up on its hind legs, it let out an ear-piercing scream and dropped heavily downwards. I ducked out of its way, but as soon as it touched the ground, the boar thrashed around like a bucking bronco.

I hurried backwards, but the boar followed. It couldn't see me — it was past seeing anything — or hear me over the sound of its roars, but somehow it followed. Turning to flee, I saw the second boar preparing itself for a charge.

I halted, momentarily unsure of myself, and the dying boar crashed into me. I fell beneath it, losing my grip on the spear. As I tried to roll over, the boar collapsed on top of me, shuddered, then went still. It was dead — and I was trapped beneath it!

I strained to push the boar off, but its weight was too much. If I'd been in good physical condition, I could have done it, but I was bruised, burnt, and bloody. I simply didn't have the strength to shift the massive animal.

As I relaxed, attempting to draw a decent breath before trying again, the second boar drew up beside me and butted my head with its own. I yelped and tried scrambling away, but couldn't. The boar seemed to grin, but that might just have been the effect of the club, which was still stuck in its mouth. It lowered its head and tried to bite me, but wasn't able, because of the club. Growling, it took a few steps back, shook its head, retreated a few more steps, then pawed the ground, lowered its tusks . . . and charged right at me.

CHAPTER SIXTEEN

I'D WRIGGLED out of some sticky situations in the past, but my luck had run out. I was trapped, at the mercy of the boar, and I knew it would show no more mercy towards me than I had shown to its partner.

As I lay, waiting for the end, eyes locked on the boar, somebody shouted loudly above me. A hush had settled over the vampires, so the voice rang clearly through the cavern: *"NO!"*

A shadow leapt into the pit, darted forward into the space between me and the boar, snatched up the spear I'd dropped, jammed the blunt end into the ground, and aimed the tip at the charging boar. The boar had no time to swerve or stop. It ran heavily onto the spear and impaled itself, then crashed into my protector, who dragged it to one side so that it wouldn't fall on me. The wrestling pair collapsed into the dust. The boar struggled weakly to get back to its feet. Lost control of its legs. Grunted feebly. Then died.

As the dust cleared, strong hands seized the boar lying on top of me and hauled its carcass out of the way. As the hands located my own and helped me to my feet, I squinted and finally realized who'd leapt to my aid — *Harkat Mulds!*

The Little Person examined me to make sure no bones were broken, then led me away from the dead boars. Above, the vampires were speechless. Then, as we made for the doors, a couple hissed. Next, a few booed. Soon the entire Hall was filled with the sound of jeers and catcalls. "Foul!" they shouted. "Disgraceful!" "Kill them both!"

Harkat and I stopped and gazed around, astonished, at the furious vampires. A short while ago they'd been hailing me as a brave-hearted warrior — now they were calling for my blood!

Not all the vampires were in an uproar. Mr. Crepsley, Gavner, and Kurda didn't raise their voices or demand justice. Nor did Seba, who I spotted sadly shaking his head and turning away.

As the vampires yelled at us, Vanez Blane stepped over the fence and climbed into the pit. He raised his hands for silence and gradually got it. "Sire!" he shouted to Mika Ver Leth, who was standing stone-faced by the fence. "I'm as appalled by this as any of you. But this wasn't planned and isn't Darren's doing. The Little Person doesn't know our ways and acted on his own. Don't hold this against us, I beg you."

Some of the vampires jeered when they heard that, but Mika Ver Leth waved sharply at them for quiet. "Darren," the Prince said slowly, "did you plan this with the Little Person?"

I shook my head. "I'm as surprised as anyone," I said.

"Harkat," Mika growled. "Did you interfere on your own account — or were you obeying orders?"

"No orders," Harkat replied. "Darren my . . . friend. Couldn't stand by . . . and watch . . . him die."

"You have defied our rules," Mika warned him.

"*Your* rules," Harkat retorted. "Not *mine*. Darren . . . friend."

The eagle-featured Mika looked troubled and ran a black-gloved finger over his upper lip as he considered the situation.

"We must kill them!" a General shouted angrily. "We must take both to the Hall of Death and —"

"Would you be so quick to kill Desmond Tiny's messenger?" Mr. Crepsley interrupted softly. The General who'd called for our heads lapsed into silence. Mr. Crepsley addressed the Hall. "We must not act hastily. This matter must be taken to the Hall of Princes, where it can be discussed reasonably. Harkat is not a vampire and cannot be judged as one. We do not have the right to pass sentence on him."

"What about the half-vampire?" another General spoke up. "*He* is subject to our laws. *He* failed the Trial and must be executed."

"He didn't fail!" Kurda shouted. "The Trial was interrupted. He'd killed one boar — who's to say he wouldn't have killed the other?"

"He was trapped!" the opposing General bellowed. "The boar was about to make a fatal charge!"

"Probably," Kurda agreed, "but we'll never know for sure. Darren proved his strength and ingenuity on previous Trials. Perhaps he would have shrugged off the dead boar and avoided the charge at the last moment."

"Nonsense!" the General snorted.

"Is it?" Kurda huffed, jumping down into the ring to join me, Harkat, and Vanez. "Can anyone say for sure that Darren would have lost?" He spun slowly, meeting the eyes of all in the Hall. "Can anyone say that he was in a truly hopeless position?"

There was a long, uneasy silence, broken in the end by a woman's voice — Arra Sails. "Kurda's right," she said. The vampires shifted uncomfortably — they hadn't expected the likes of Arra to side with Kurda. "The boy's situation was perilous, but not necessarily fatal. He *might* have survived."

"I say Darren has the right to retake the Trial," Kurda said, seizing on the uncertain silence that filled the Hall. "We should adjourn and stage it again, tomorrow."

Everybody looked to Mika Ver Leth for judgment. The Prince brooded on the matter in silence some moments, then glanced at Mr. Crepsley. "Larten? What do you say about this?"

Mr. Crepsley shrugged grimly. "It is true that Darren was not actually defeated. But breaking the rules usually means a forfeit. My relationship with Darren forces me to speak for him. Alas, I do not know how to make a case for mercy. Whatever the circumstances, he has failed the Trial."

"Larten!" Kurda screeched. "You don't know what you're saying!"

"Yes, he does," I sighed. "And he's right." Pushing Harkat away, I stood by myself and faced Mika Ver Leth. "I don't think I'd have escaped," I said honestly. "I don't want to die, but I won't ask for any special favors. If it's possible to take the Trial again, I will. If not, I won't complain."

An approving murmur ran through the Hall.

Those who'd been standing angrily by the fence settled back and waited for Mika to make his call. "You speak like a true vampire," the Prince praised me. "I do not blame you for what happened. Nor do I blame your friend — he is not one of us and cannot be expected to act as we do. There will be no measures taken against Harkat Mulds — that is a guarantee I am willing to make here and now, on my own."

Some of the vampires glared at Harkat, but none raised a voice against him. "As for *your* fate," Mika said, then hesitated. "I must speak with my fellow Princes and Generals before passing sentence. I don't think your life can be spared, but Kurda may have a point — perhaps it *is* possible to take the Trial again. To the best of my knowledge, it has never been permitted, but maybe there's an old law we can fall back on.

"Return to your cell," Mika said, "while I and the others consult with our colleagues. You'll be informed of our decision as soon as we reach one. My advice," he added in a whisper, "would be to make your peace with the gods, for I fear you will face them shortly."

I nodded obediently to Mika Ver Leth and kept my head bowed while he and the other vampires filed from the Hall.

"I won't let you perish without a fight," Kurda

promised as he slipped past me. "You'll get out of this yet, I'm sure of it. There must be a way."

Then he was gone. So were Vanez Blane, Mr. Crepsley, and the rest, leaving just me and Harkat with the dead boars in the pit. Harkat looked shameful when I turned and faced him. "I did not . . . mean to . . . cause trouble," he said. "I acted . . . before I could . . . think."

"Don't worry about it," I told him. "I'd probably have done the same thing if I was in your place. Besides, the worst they can do is kill me — I'd have died anyway if you hadn't leapt to my rescue."

"You are . . . not angry?" Harkat asked.

"Of course not." I smiled, and we started for the exit.

What I didn't say to Harkat was that I wished he *had* left me to die. At least with the boar, my death would have been fast and easy to face. Now I had a long, nervous wait, which would almost certainly be followed by a gut-wrenching walk to the Hall of Death, where I'd be hoisted above the stakes and subjected to a messy, painful, and humiliating end. It would have been better to die nobly and quickly in the pit.

CHAPTER SEVENTEEN

HARKAT AND I sat on our hammocks and waited. The neighboring cells were deserted, as were the tunnels. Most of the vampires had gathered in the Hall of Princes or were waiting outside for the verdict — vampires loved intrigue almost as much as they loved fighting, and all were anxious to hear the news firsthand.

"How come you leapt to my rescue?" I asked Harkat after a while, to break the nerve-racking silence. "You might have been killed trying to save me."

"To be honest," Harkat replied sheepishly, "I acted . . . for my own sake . . . not yours. If you die, I might . . . never find out . . . who I used . . . to be."

I laughed. "You'd better not tell the vampires that. The only reason they've gone lightly on you is that they respect bravery and self-sacrifice. If they learn you did it to save your own skin, there's no telling what they'd do!"

"You do not . . . mind?" Harkat asked.

"No." I smiled.

"If they decide . . . to kill you, will you . . . let them?"

"I won't be able to stop them," I answered.

"But will you . . . go quietly?"

"I'm not sure," I sighed. "If they'd taken me right after the fight, I'd have gone without a murmur — I was pumped up with adrenaline and wasn't scared of dying. Now that I've calmed down, I'm dreading it. I hope I'll go with my head held high, but I'm afraid I'll cry and beg for mercy."

"Not you," Harkat said. "You're too . . . tough."

"You think?" I laughed dryly.

"You fought . . . boars and faced . . . fire and water. You didn't . . . show fear before. Why should . . . you now?"

"That was different," I said. "I had a fighting chance. If they decide to kill me, I'll have to walk to the Hall of Death *knowing* it's all over."

"Don't worry," Harkat said. "If you do . . . die, maybe you . . . will come back . . . as a Little . . . Person."

I stared at Harkat's misshapen body, his scarred,

disfigured face, his green eyes, and the mask he couldn't survive without. "Oh, that's a great comfort," I said sarcastically.

"Just trying . . . to cheer you up."

"Well, don't!"

Minutes trickled by agonizingly. I wished the vampires would reach their decision quickly, even if it meant death — anything would be better than sitting here, not knowing. Finally, after what felt like a lifetime, there came the sound of feet in the tunnel outside. Harkat and I tensed, rolled off our hammocks, and jumped to attention by the door of the cell. We glanced nervously at each other. Harkat grinned weakly. My grin was even weaker.

"Here we go," I whispered.

"Good luck," he replied.

The footsteps slowed, stopped, then came again, softly. A vampire emerged from the gloom of the tunnel and slid into the cell — Kurda.

"What's happening?" I asked.

"I came to see how you were doing," he said, smiling crookedly.

"Fine!" I snapped. "Just dandy. Couldn't be better."

"I thought as much." He looked around twitchily.

"Have they . . . decided yet?" Harkat asked.

"No. But it won't be long. They . . ." — He cleared his throat — "They're going to demand your death, Darren."

I'd been expecting it, but it hit me hard all the same. I took a step backwards, and my knees buckled. If Harkat hadn't caught and steadied me, I would have fallen.

"I've tried arguing them out of it," Kurda said. "Others have too — Gavner and Vanez put their careers on the line to plead for you. But there aren't any precedents. The laws are clear — failure to complete the Trials must be punished with death. We tried convincing the Princes to let you take the Trial again, but they turned a deaf ear to our pleas."

"So why haven't they come for me?" I asked.

"They're still debating. Larten's been calling older vampires forward and asking if they ever heard of something like this happening before. He's trying hard for you. If there's the slightest legal loophole, he'll find it."

"But there isn't, is there?" I asked glumly.

Kurda shook his head. "If Paris Skyle knows of no way to save you, I'm sure none of the others do either. If he can't help you, I doubt that anyone can."

"So it's over. I'm finished."

"Not necessarily," Kurda said, averting his eyes, strangely embarrassed.

"I don't understand." I frowned. "You just said —"

"The verdict's inevitable," he interrupted. "That doesn't mean you have to stay and face it."

"Kurda!" I gasped, appalled by what he was saying.

"You can get out," he whispered. "I know a way past the guards, a breach point I never informed anybody about. We can take rarely used tunnels down through the mountain, to save time. Dawn isn't far off. Once you get out in the open, you'll have a free run until dusk. Even then, I don't think anybody will come after you. Since you don't pose a threat, they'll let you go. They might kill you if they run into you later, but for the time being —"

"I couldn't do that," I interrupted. "Mr. Crepsley would be ashamed of me. I'm his assistant. He'd have to answer for it."

"No," Kurda said. "You're not his responsibility, not since you embarked on the Trials. People might say things behind his back, but nobody would question his good name out in the open."

"I couldn't," I said again, with less conviction this time. "What about *you*? If they found out you'd helped me escape . . ."

"They won't," Kurda said. "I'll cover my tracks. As long as you aren't caught, I'll be fine."

"And if I *am* caught, and they worm the truth out of me?"

Kurda shrugged. "I'll take that chance."

I hesitated, torn by uncertainty. The vampire part of me wanted to stay and take what I had coming. The human part said not to be a fool, grab my opportunity and run.

"You're young, Darren," Kurda said. "It's crazy to throw your life away. Leave Vampire Mountain. Make a fresh start. You're experienced enough to survive on your own. You don't need Larten to look after you anymore. Lots of vampires lead their own lives, having nothing to do with the rest of us. Be your own person. Don't let the foolish pride of others cloud your judgment."

"What do *you* think?" I asked Harkat.

"I think . . . Kurda's right," he said. "No point . . . letting them kill . . . you. Go. Live. Be free. I will . . . come with you . . . and help. Later, maybe *you* . . . can help *me*."

"Harkat won't be able to come," Kurda said. "He's too broad to fit through some of the tunnels I plan to use. You can arrange to meet somewhere else, when Council is over and he's free to leave without drawing suspicion to himself."

"The Cirque . . . Du Freak," Harkat said. "You'll be able . . . to find it?"

I nodded. I'd gotten to know a lot of people around the world during my years with the Cirque, people who assisted Mr. Tall and his colleagues when they came to town. They'd be able to point me in the direction of the traveling circus.

"Have you decided?" Kurda asked. "There's no time to stand and debate the issue. Come with me now, or stay to face your death."

I gulped deeply, stared at my feet, came to a decision, then locked gazes with Kurda and said, "I'll come." I wasn't proud of myself, but shame was a lot sweeter than the sharpened stakes in the Hall of Death.

CHAPTER EIGHTEEN

WE HURRIED through the deserted corridors, down to the storerooms. Kurda led me to the back of one, where we moved aside a couple of large sacks, revealing a small hole in the wall. Kurda began to squeeze through, but I pulled him back and asked if we could rest for a couple of minutes — I was in a lot of pain.

"Will you be able to continue?" he asked.

"Yes, but only if we stop for regular breaks. I know time is precious, but I'm too exhausted to keep going without resting."

When I felt ready, I followed Kurda through the hole and found myself in a cramped tunnel that dropped sharply. I suggested we slide to the bottom, but Kurda rejected the idea. "We're not going all the way down," he said. "There's a shelf halfway down this hole that leads to another tunnel."

Sure enough, after several minutes we came to a ledge, left the hole, and were soon back on level ground. "How did you find this place?" I asked.

"I followed a bat," he said, and winked.

We came to a fork, and Kurda stopped to get out a map. He studied it silently for a few seconds, then took the turn to the left.

"Are you sure you know where you're going?" I asked.

"Not entirely." He laughed. "That's why I brought my maps. I haven't been down some of these tunnels in decades."

I tried keeping track of the route we were taking, in case anything happened to Kurda, and I had to find my way back on my own, but it was impossible. We twisted and turned so many times, only a genius could have memorized the way.

We passed over a couple of small streams. Kurda told me that they joined up with others farther ahead, to form the wide stream that had been used for burying the dead in the past. "We could always swim to safety," I suggested jokingly.

"Why not flap our arms and fly away while we're at it?" Kurda replied.

Some of the tunnels were pitch black, but Kurda didn't light any candles — he said the wax droppings would mark our trail and make it easy for pursuing vampires to track us.

The father we progressed, the harder it became for me to keep up, and we had to stop often so I could catch my breath and work up the energy to continue.

"I'd carry you if there was room," Kurda said during one of our rest periods, wiping sweat and blood from my neck and shoulders with his shirt. "We'll be entering larger tunnels shortly. I can give you a boost then if you'd like."

"That'd be great," I wheezed.

"What about when we get out of the tunnels?" he asked. "Do you want me to come with you some of the way, to make sure you're OK?"

I shook my head. "You'd be discovered by the Generals if you did. I'll be fine once I get outside. The fresh air will perk me up. I'll find somewhere to sleep, rest for a few hours, then —"

I stopped. Loose pebbles had clattered to the floor in one of the tunnels behind us. Kurda heard them too. He ran to the mouth of the tunnel and squatted by the opening, listening intently. After a few seconds, he raced back to my side. "Someone's coming!" he hissed, dragging me to my feet. "Hurry! We must get out of here!"

"No," I sighed, sitting down again.

"Darren!" he screeched softly. "You can't stay. We've got to make a break for it before —"

"I can't," I told him. "Shuffling was hard enough — there's no way I can take part in a full-speed chase. If we've been found, that's the end. Go on ahead and hide. I'll pretend I acted alone."

"You know I wouldn't leave you," he said, squatting beside me.

We waited in silence as the footsteps came closer. By the sound, there was only one person following us. I hoped it wasn't Mr. Crepsley — I dreaded the thought of facing him after what I'd done.

The tracking vampire reached the mouth of the tunnel, studied us from the shadows a moment, then ducked forward and hurried over. It was Gavner Purl! "You two are in *so* much trouble," he snarled. "Whose dumb idea was it to run?"

"Mine!" Kurda and I said at the exact same time.

Gavner shook his head, exasperated. "You're as bad as each other," he snapped. "Come on — the truth."

"It was my idea," Kurda answered, squeezing my arm to silence my protestations. "I persuaded Darren to come. The blame is mine."

"You're an idiot," Gavner reprimanded him. "This will destroy you if word gets out. You won't just have to forget about becoming a Vampire Prince — chances are you'll be carted off to the Hall of Death to suffer the same fate as Darren."

"Only if you tell on me," Kurda said quietly.

"You think I won't?" Gavner challenged him.

"If it was your intention to punish us, you wouldn't have come alone."

Gavner stared at the senior vampire, then cursed shortly. "You're right," he groaned. "I don't want to see you killed. If the two of you come back with me, I'll keep your name out of it. In fact, nobody ever need know it happened. Harkat and I are the only ones who know at the moment. We can get Darren back before judgment is passed."

"Why?" Kurda asked. "So he can be taken to the Hall of Death and impaled?"

"If that's the judgment of the Princes — yes," Gavner said.

Kurda shook his head. "That's what we're escaping from. I won't let him go back to be killed. It's wrong to take a boy's life in such a heartless fashion."

"Wrong or right," Gavner snapped, "the judgment of the Princes is final!"

Kurda narrowed his eyes. "You agree with me," he whispered. "You think his life should be spared."

Gavner nodded reluctantly. "But that's my own

opinion. I'm not going to ignore the ruling of the Princes."

"Why not?" Kurda asked. "Do we have to obey them even when they're wrong, even when they rule unjustly?"

"It's our way," Gavner growled.

"Ways can be changed," Kurda insisted. "The Princes are too inflexible. They ignore the fact that the world is moving forward. In a few weeks, *I'll* be a Prince. I can change things. Let Darren go, and I'll get the ruling against him overturned. I'll clear his name and allow him to return and complete his Trials. Turn a blind eye just this once and I swear you won't regret it."

Gavner was troubled by Kurda's words. "It's wrong to plot against the Princes," he muttered.

"Nobody will know," Kurda promised. "They'll think Darren got away by himself. We'll never be investigated."

"It goes against everything we believe in," Gavner sighed.

"Sometimes we have to abandon old beliefs in favor of new ones," Kurda said.

While Gavner agonized over his decision, I spoke up. "I'll go back if you want me to. I'm afraid of dying, which is why I let Kurda talk me into fleeing. But if you say I should return, I will."

"I don't *want* you to die," Gavner cried. "But running away never solved anything."

"Nonsense!" Kurda snorted. "Vampires would be a lot better off if more of us had the good sense to run from a fight when the odds are stacked against us. If we take Darren back, we take him back to die. Where's the sense in that?"

Gavner thought it over in silence, then nodded morosely. "I don't like it, but it's the lesser of two evils. I won't turn you in. But," he added, "only if you agree to present the truth to the others once you become a Prince. We'll come clean, clear Darren's name if we can, accept our punishment if we can't. OK?"

"That's fine by me," Kurda said.

"Your word on it?"

Kurda nodded. "My word."

Gavner let out a long breath and studied me in the gloom of the tunnel. "How are you anyway?" he asked.

"Not so bad," I lied.

"You look like you're about to drop," he noted skeptically.

"I'll make it," I vowed. Then I asked how he'd found us.

"I went looking for Kurda," he explained. "I was hoping we could put our heads together and figure a way out of this mess. His map cabinet was open. I didn't think anything of it at the time, but when I dropped by your cell and found Harkat there by himself, I put two and two together."

"How did you track us through the tunnels?" Kurda asked.

Gavner pointed to a drop of blood on the floor beneath me. "He's been dripping the whole way," he said. "He's left a trail even a fool could follow."

Kurda closed his eyes and grimaced. "Charna's guts! Espionage never was my strong suit."

"You're right!" Gavner snorted. "If we're going to pull this off, we'd better move quickly. As soon as Darren's discovered missing, there'll be a team of trackers on his trail, and it won't take them long to find him. Our only chance is to get him outside and hope the sun prevents them from continuing."

"My thoughts exactly," Kurda said, and started ahead. I followed as well as I could, Gavner puffing along behind.

At the end of the tunnel, Kurda turned left. I headed after him, but Gavner grabbed my arm and stopped me, then studied the tunnel to his right. When Kurda realized we weren't at his heels, he paused and looked back. "What's the delay?" he asked.

"I've been in this part of the mountain before,"

Gavner said. "It was during my Trials of Initiation. I had to find a hidden jewel."

"So?"

"I can find the way out," Gavner said. "I know the path to the nearest exit."

"So do I," Kurda said, "and it's this way."

Gavner shook his head. "We *can* get out that way," he agreed, "but it'll be quicker if we take this other tunnel."

"No!" Kurda snapped. "This was my idea. I'm in charge. We don't have time to go wandering around. If you're wrong, it'll cost us. My way is certain."

"So's mine," Gavner insisted, and before Kurda could object, he ducked down the tunnel to the right, dragging me along after him. Kurda cursed loudly and called us back, but when Gavner ignored him, he had no choice other than to hurry after us.

"This is stupid," Kurda panted when he caught up. He tried to squeeze past me to deal with Gavner face-to-face, but the tunnel was too narrow. "We should stick to the route on the maps. I know more about these tunnels than you. There's nothing the way you're going except dead ends."

"No," Gavner contradicted him. "We can save almost forty minutes this way."

"But what if —," Kurda began.

"Stop arguing," Gavner interrupted. "The more we talk, the slower we progress."

Kurda muttered something, but said no more about it. I could tell he wasn't happy though.

We passed through a small tunnel that cut beneath a roaring mountain stream. The water sounded so close, I was afraid it might break through the walls of the tunnel and flood us. I couldn't hear anything over the noise of the stream, and it was so dark, I couldn't see anything either. It felt as if I was all alone.

I was delighted to finally see light at the end, and hurried towards it as fast as I could. Gavner and Kurda also moved quickly, so they must have been anxious to escape the tunnel too. As we brushed the dirt from the tunnel off ourselves, Kurda moved ahead and took the lead. We were in a small cave. There were three tunnels leading out of it. Kurda went to the tunnel on the far left. "We're taking this one," he said, re-exerting his authority.

Gavner grinned. "That's the one I planned to take anyway."

"Then hurry up," Kurda snapped.

"What's wrong with you?" Gavner asked. "You're acting oddly."

"No, I'm not!" Kurda glared, then smiled weakly. "Sorry. It's that tunnel under the stream. I knew we'd have to pass through it. That's why I wanted to go the other way — to avoid it."

"Afraid the water would break through?" Gavner laughed.

"Yes," Kurda answered stiffly.

"I was afraid too," I said. "I wouldn't like to crawl through a place like that too often."

"Cowards." Gavner chuckled. He started towards Kurda, smiling, then stopped and turned his head sideways.

"What's wrong?" I asked.

"I thought I heard something," he said.

"What?"

"It sounded like someone coughing. It came from the tunnel to the right."

"A search party?" I asked worriedly.

Gavner frowned. "I doubt it — they'd be coming from behind."

"What's going on?" Kurda asked impatiently.

"Gavner thinks he heard something," I said as the General crept across to explore the tunnel.

"It's just the sound of the stream," Kurda said. "We don't have time to —"

But it was too late. Gavner had already entered the tunnel. Kurda hurried over to where I was standing and peered into the darkness of the tunnel after

Gavner. "We'd be better off on our own," he grumbled. "He's done nothing but slow us down."

"What if somebody's in there?" I asked.

"There's nobody down here besides us," Kurda snorted. "We should head on without that fool and leave him to catch up."

"No," I said, "I'd rather wait."

Kurda rolled his eyes but stood sullenly beside me. Gavner was gone no more than a couple of minutes, but when he returned he looked years older. His legs were shaking, and he sank to his bottom as soon as he emerged from the tunnel.

"What's wrong?" I asked.

He shook his head wordlessly.

"You found something?" Kurda asked.

"There's . . ." Gavner cleared his throat. "Go look," he whispered. "But be careful. Don't be seen."

"Seen by who?" I asked, but he didn't answer.

Curious, I crept along the tunnel, Kurda right behind me. It was short, and as I approached the end, I noticed the flicker of torches in a large cave beyond. I dropped to my stomach, then edged forward so that I had a clear view of the cave. What I saw froze my guts inside me.

Twenty or thirty people were lounging around. Some were sitting, some lying on mats, some playing cards. They had the general appearance of vampires — bulky, rough features, crude haircuts. But I could see their purplish skin and reddish hair and eyes, and I identified them immediately — our blood foes, *the vampaneze!*

CHAPTER NINETEEN

KURDA AND I retreated slowly and joined Gavner in the smaller cave. We sat next to him and nobody said anything for a while. Finally Gavner spoke in a dull, distracted tone. "I counted thirty-four of them."

"There were thirty-five when we looked," Kurda said.

"There are two adjoining caves of similar size," Gavner noted. "There might be more in those."

"What are they doing here?" I asked in a whisper.

The vampires trained their sights on me.

"Why do you *think* they're here?" Gavner asked.

I licked my lips nervously. "To attack us?" I guessed.

"You got it," Gavner said grimly.

"Not necessarily," Kurda said. "They might have come to discuss a treaty."

"You think so?" Gavner sneered.

"No," Kurda sighed. "Not really."

"We have to warn the vampires," I said.

Kurda nodded. "But what about your escape? One of us can lead you to —"

"Forget it," I interrupted. "I'm not running away from something like this."

"Come on then," Kurda said, getting to his feet and making for the tunnel under the stream. "The quicker we tell the others, the quicker we can return and —" He was bending down to enter the tunnel, but stopped suddenly and spun to the side. Signaling us to stay where we were, he peered cautiously into the tunnel, then raced back. "Somebody's coming!" he hissed.

"Vampires or vampaneze?" Gavner asked.

"Too dark to tell. Think we can afford to wait and find out?"

"No," Gavner said. "We've got to get out of here." He studied the three exit tunnels. "We can get back to the Halls by the middle tunnel, but it'll take a lot of time. If they spot Darren's trail of blood and come after us . . ."

"We'll take the left tunnel," Kurda said.

"That doesn't lead up." Gavner frowned.

"According to my maps, it does," Kurda contradicted him. "There's a very small connecting tunnel, easy to miss. I only found it by chance."

"You're sure?" Gavner asked.

"Maps don't lie," Kurda said.

"Then let's go," Gavner decided, and off we dashed.

I forgot about my pain as we sped through the tunnels. There was no time to worry about myself. The entire vampire clan was under threat, and all I thought about was getting back to the Hall of Princes and tipping them off.

When we reached Kurda's connecting tunnel, we discovered a cave-in. We stared at the pile of rocks, dismayed, then Kurda swore and kicked angrily at the blockage.

"I'm sorry," he sighed.

"It's not your fault," Gavner told him. "You couldn't have known."

"Where do we go now?" I asked.

"Back through the cave?" Gavner suggested.

Kurda shook his head. "If we've been discovered, they'll come after us that way. There's another tunnel we can use. It'll take us back in the same direction, and it links up with tunnels leading to the Halls."

"Let's go then," Gavner barked, and we followed after Kurda as he led the way through the dark.

We spoke as little as possible, pausing occasionally to listen for sounds of pursuit. There weren't any, but that didn't mean we weren't being hunted — vampaneze can move as silently as vampires when they wish.

After a while, Kurda came to a stop and pressed his head close to ours. "We're right behind the cave where the vampaneze are," he whispered. "Move slowly and carefully. If they spot us, fight for your lives — then run like hell!"

"Wait," I said. "I don't have a weapon. I'll need one if we're attacked."

"I only have one knife," Kurda said. "Gavner?"

"I have two, but I'll need both of them."

"So what will I fight with?" I hissed. "Bad breath?"

Gavner grinned grimly. "No offense, Darren, but if Kurda and I can't fend them off, I don't think you can make much of a difference. If we run into trouble, grab Kurda's maps and head for the Halls while we stay and fight."

"I couldn't do that," I gasped.

"You'll do as you're told," Gavner growled, leaving no room for argument.

We started forward again, softer than ever. Sounds from the cave reached our ears — vampaneze laughing and talking quietly. If I'd been alone, I might have panicked and bolted, but Kurda and Gavner were made of sterner stuff, and their calm presence held me in check.

Our luck held until we turned into a long tunnel and ran into a lone vampaneze, walking towards us, fiddling with his belt. He glanced up casually as we froze, saw in an instant that we weren't vampaneze, and opened his mouth to roar.

Gavner darted forward, knives flashing. He stuck one deep into the vampaneze's belly and slashed the other across his throat before he could make a sound and alert his companions. It had been a close call, and we were all smiling weakly with relief as Gavner laid the dead body on the ground. But as we were about to move on, another vampaneze appeared at the far end of the tunnel, saw us, and yelled for help.

Gavner groaned desolately. "So much for stealth," he muttered as vampaneze poured in from the cavern. He took a firm stand in the middle of the tunnel, checked the walls on each side, then spoke over his shoulder. "You two get out of here. I'll delay them as long as I can."

"I won't leave you to face them alone," Kurda said.

"You will if you have any brains," Gavner snarled.

"This tunnel's narrow. One person can hold them off as easily as two. Take Darren and break for the Halls, as fast as you can."

"But —," Kurda started to say.

"You're arguing our chances away!" Gavner roared, flicking a knife at one of the nearest vampaneze, forcing him back. "Move that dead vampaneze from behind me, so I don't trip over him — and run!"

Kurda nodded sadly. "Luck, Gavner Purl," he said.

"Luck," Gavner grunted, and made another attack.

We dragged the dead body out of Gavner's way and retreated to the mouth of the tunnel. Kurda paused there and studied Gavner in silence as he sliced at the vampaneze with his pair of knives. He was keeping them at arm's length, but it would be only a matter of minutes before they swarmed over him, took his weapons, and killed him.

Kurda turned to lead me away, then stopped and dug out a map. "Do you remember the old burial chamber we visited?" he asked. "The Hall of Final Voyage?"

"Yes," I said.

"Do you think you could find your way back to the Halls from it?"

"Probably."

He stuck the map away and pointed down the tunnel we were in. "Go to the end of this," he said. "Take a right, another right, then four lefts. That'll bring you to the chamber. Wait a few minutes in case one of us comes. Get your breath back. Try rebandaging yourself so that you stop dripping blood. Then go."

"What are you going to do?" I asked.

"Help Gavner."

"But he said —"

"I know what he said!" Kurda snapped. "I don't care. Two of us working together stand a better chance of holding them." Kurda gripped my shoulders and squeezed tightly. "Luck, Darren Shan."

"Luck," I replied miserably.

"Don't stay and watch," he said. "Leave immediately."

"OK," I agreed, and slipped away.

I got as far as the second right turn before I stopped. I knew I should do as Kurda said and flee for the Halls, but I couldn't bear the thought of leaving my friends behind. They were in this mess because of me. It would have been unfair to leave them to face death while I waltzed away scot-free. *Somebody* had to warn the vampires, but I didn't think it should be me. If I told Kurda I'd forgotten the way back, he'd have to go himself, meaning I could stay and fight beside Gavner.

I backtracked to the tunnel where the fighting was raging. When I got there, I saw that Gavner was still holding the vampaneze off single-handedly. Kurda hadn't been able to move forward. The two were arguing. "I told you to leave!" Gavner roared.

"And I'm telling you I won't!" Kurda shrieked back.

"What about Darren?"

"I gave him directions to get back."

"You're a fool, Kurda," Gavner shouted.

"I know," Kurda laughed. "Now, are you going to let me in for a piece of this, or do I have to fight you as well as the vampaneze?"

Gavner stabbed at a vampaneze who had a round, dark red birthmark on his left cheek, then dropped back a few steps. "OK," he grunted. "The next time there's a break in the fighting, move up to my right."

"Agreed," Kurda said, and held his knife tightly by his side while he waited.

I crept forward. I didn't want to yell and distract them. I was almost upon them when the vampaneze fell back several feet and Gavner shouted, "Now!"

Gavner edged to his left, and Kurda moved forward, filling the space beside him. I realized it was too late for me to take Kurda's place, so I started to turn away reluctantly. As I did, something crazy happened that stopped me dead in my tracks and held me rooted to the spot.

As Kurda stepped up beside Gavner, he raised his knife high and swung it down in a vicious arc. It cut deep into the belly of its intended target, slicing open the flesh, ensuring death. It would have been a lovely stroke to behold if it had been directed at one of the vampaneze. But Kurda hadn't stuck the blade into any of the purple-skinned invaders — he'd stuck it into *Gavner Purl!*

CHAPTER TWENTY

I COULDN'T understand what was happening. Neither could Gavner. He slumped against the wall and stared at the knife sticking out of his belly. He dropped his own knives, gripped the handle, and tried to pull it out, but his strength deserted him, and he slid to the floor.

Though Gavner and I were shocked, the vampaneze didn't seem the least bit surprised. They relaxed, and those at the rear returned to their cave. The one with the red birthmark on his cheek stepped forward, stood beside Kurda, and studied the dying vampire. "I thought for a minute you were coming to his aid," the vampaneze said.

"No," Kurda replied. He sounded mournful. "I'd have knocked him out and taken him away somewhere if possible, but others could have tracked down his mental signals. There's a boy up ahead, a half-vampire. He's injured, so he won't be hard to catch. I want him taken alive. They won't be able to track him."

"Do you mean the boy behind you?" the vampaneze asked.

Kurda swiveled sharply. "Darren!" he gasped. "How long have you been there? How much have you —"

Gavner groaned. I jolted into action, ducked forward, ignored Kurda and the vampaneze, and crouched beside my dying friend. His eyes were wide open but he didn't seem to see anything. "Gavner?" I asked, holding his hands, which were bloody from trying to take out the knife. The Vampire General coughed and trembled. I could feel the life slipping out of him. "I'm with you, Gavner," I whispered, crying. "You're not alone. I'll —"

"Suh-suh-suh," he stuttered.

"What is it?" I wept. "Don't hurry. You've got plenty of time." That was a barefaced lie.

"Suh-sorry if muh-muh-my snoring . . . kuh-kept you . . . awake," he wheezed. I didn't know if the words were meant for me or someone else, and before I could ask, his expression froze on his face, and his spirit passed on to Paradise.

I pressed my forehead to Gavner's and howled pitifully, clutching his dead body to mine. The vampaneze could have taken me easily then, but they were embarrassed, and nobody moved forward to capture me. They just stood around, waiting for me to stop crying.

When I finally raised my head, nobody dared meet my gaze. All eyes dropped to the floor, Kurda's quickest of all. "You killed him!" I hissed.

Kurda gulped deeply. "I had to," he croaked. "There was no time to let him die a noble death — you might have gotten away if I'd left him for the vampaneze."

"You knew they were here all along," I whispered.

He nodded. "That's why I didn't want to take the route under the stream," he said. "I feared this would happen. Everything would have been OK if we'd gone the way I wanted."

"You're in league with them!" I shouted. "You're a *traitor!*"

"You don't understand what's happening," he sighed. "This looks terrible, but it's not what you think. I'm trying to *save* our race, not condemn it. There are things you don't know — things *no* vampire knows. Gavner's death is regrettable, but when I explain prop —"

"The hell with your explanations!" I screamed. "You're a traitor and a murderer — scum!"

"I saved your life," Kurda reminded me gently.

"At the expense of Gavner's," I sobbed. "Why did you do it? He was your friend. He . . ." I shook my head and stopped myself before he could answer. "Never mind. I don't want to hear." Stooping, I picked up one of Gavner's knives and brandished it in front of me. The vampaneze raised their weapons immediately and closed in.

"No!" Kurda shouted, stepping in their way. "I said I wanted him taken alive!"

"He has a knife," the vampaneze with the birthmark growled. "Do you want us to let him chop off our fingers while we get it away from him?"

"Don't worry, Glalda," Kurda said. "I'm in control of the situation." Dropping his knife, he spread his hands and walked slowly towards me.

"Stop!" I yelled. "Don't come any closer!"

"I'm unarmed," he said.

"I don't care. I'll kill you anyway. You deserve it."

"Maybe so," Kurda agreed, "but I don't think you'd kill an unarmed man, no matter what he'd done. If I'm wrong, I'll pay for my error of judgment in the severest way possible — but I don't think I am."

I drew back the knife to stab him, then lowered my hand. He was right — even though he'd killed Gavner in cold blood, I couldn't bring myself to do the same.

"I hate you!" I cried, then threw my knife at him. As he ducked, I spun and sped back up the tunnel, turned right, and fled.

As the vampaneze surged after me, I heard Kurda roaring at them not to harm me. He told them I was injured and couldn't get far. One roared back that he was cutting ahead with a few others to block off the tunnels leading to the Halls. Another wanted to know if I was carrying any other weapons.

Then I passed out of earshot of the enemies and the traitor and was racing through darkness, fleeing blindly, crying for my sacrificed friend — the poor, dead Gavner Purl.

CHAPTER TWENTY-ONE

THE VAMPANEZE took their time hunting me down. They knew I couldn't escape. I was injured and tired, so all they had to do was stay close and slowly reel me in. As I scurried and twisted through the tunnels, the roar of the mountain stream increased, and I realized my feet were guiding me to the old burial chamber. I thought about changing direction, to outwit Kurda, but I'd lose my way if I did and never make it back to the Halls. My only chance was to take the paths I was familiar with and hope I could block one off by bringing down the ceiling behind me.

I burst into the Hall of Final Voyage and paused to catch my breath. I could hear the sounds of the vampaneze behind. They were far too close for comfort. I needed to rest but there was no time. Struggling to my feet, I looked for the way out.

At first the cave seemed unfamiliar, and I wondered if I'd possibly wandered into the wrong one by mistake. Then it struck me that I was simply on the side of the stream opposite where I'd been before. Advancing to the edge of the bank, I looked across and saw the tunnel I needed to leave by. I also saw a very pale-skinned person with white eyes and rags for clothes, sitting on a rock close to the wall — a Guardian of the Blood!

"Help," I shouted, startling the thin man, who leapt to his feet and squinted at me. "Vampaneze!" I croaked. "They've invaded the mountain. You've got to warn the Generals!"

The Guardian's eyes narrowed, and he shook his head, then said something in a language I didn't understand. I opened my mouth to repeat the warning, but before I could, he made a sign with his fingers, shook his head again, and slipped out of the cave, disappearing swiftly into the shadows of the tunnel beyond.

I cursed — the Guardians of the Blood must also be in league with the vampaneze! — then glanced down into the dark water at my feet and shivered. The stream wasn't particularly wide, and I could have jumped it with ease any other time. But I was exhausted, aching, and desperate. All I wanted to do was lie down and let the vampaneze have me. Going on seemed pointless. They were sure to catch me. It would be a lot easier to surrender now and . . .

"No!" I shouted aloud. They killed Gavner, and they'd kill the rest of the vampires — including Mr. Crepsley — if I couldn't get to the Halls first and stop them. I *had* to go on. I took a few steps back, preparing for the jump. Looking over my shoulder, I saw the first of the vampaneze enter the cave. I backed up a few more steps, then raced to the edge of the bank and leapt.

I knew immediately that I wasn't going to make it. There hadn't been enough pace or spring in my step. I flailed out with my arms, in the hope of catching hold of the ledge, but fell several feet shy of safety and dropped into the freezing water of the stream.

The current caught me instantly. By the time I bobbed to the surface, the mouth of the tunnel leading out of the cave and back underground was almost upon me. I threw out my arms, terrified, and caught hold of a rock jutting out of the bank. Using the last of my strength, I clawed my way to partial safety. Defying the flow of the water, I half-flopped onto the rock and grabbed hold of some deep-rooted weeds.

It was a perilous position, but I might have been able to scrape my way out of it — if not for the dozen or so vampaneze who'd crossed the stream and were standing overhead, arms folded, waiting patiently. One lit a cigarette, then flicked his match at my face. It missed, hit the water, quenched with a hiss, and disappeared at a frightening speed down the dark tunnel into the mountain.

As I clung to the rock, frozen and soaking, wondering what to do, Kurda pushed his way through the vampaneze and dropped to his knees. He extended a hand to help me up, but couldn't reach. "Somebody grab my ankles and lower me," he said.

"Why?" the vampaneze named Glalda asked. "Let him drown. It'll be easier."

"No!" Kurda barked. "His death serves no purpose. He's young and open to new ideas. We'll need vampires like him if we're going to —"

"OK, OK," Glalda sighed, and signaled two of his men to take Kurda's legs and lower him over the edge, so that he could rescue me.

I stared at Kurda's hands as they stretched towards my own, then at his face, mere inches away. "You killed Gavner," I snarled.

"We'll discuss that later," he said, snatching at my wrists.

I pulled my hands out of his way and spat on his fingers, even though I nearly fell back into the water. I couldn't bear the thought of him touching me. "Why did you do it?" I moaned.

Kurda shook his head. "It's too complicated. Come with me and I'll explain later. When you're safe, dry, and fed, I'll sit you down and —"

"Don't touch me!" I screeched as he reached for me again.

"Don't be stupid," he said. "You're in no position to argue. Take my hand and let me pull you to safety. You won't be harmed, I promise."

"You *promise*," I sneered. "Your word means nothing. You're a liar and a traitor. I wouldn't believe you if you said the world was round."

"Believe what you want," he snapped, "but I'm all that stands between you and a watery grave, so you can't afford to be picky. Take my hand and stop acting like an idiot."

"You have no clue," I said, shaking my head in disgust. "You don't know a thing about honor or loyalty. I'd rather die than give myself up to scum like you."

"Don't be —," Kurda started to say, but before he could finish, I released my grip on the rock, pushed backwards with my legs, and let the water have me. "Darren — no!" Kurda screamed, making one last grab for me. But he was too late — his fingers clutched at thin air.

I drifted out into the middle of the stream, beyond the reach of Kurda and his vampaneze allies. There was a moment of strange peace, during which I bobbed up and down in the center of the stream. Locking gazes with Kurda as I hung there, I smiled thinly and pressed the middle fingers of my right hand to my forehead and eyelids, making the death's touch sign. "Even in death, may I be triumphant!" I howled, adding a quick silent prayer that my curse would ring true, and that my sacrifice would encourage the gods of the vampires to extract a terrible revenge on this traitor and his allies.

Then, before Kurda could respond, the current took hold and swept me away in a brutal instant, out of his sight, into darkness, churning madness, and the hungry belly of the mountain.

TO BE CONTINUED . . .

THE VAMPIRE PRINCE

DARKNESS — COLD — churning water — roaring, like a thousand lions — spinning around and around — bashing into rocks — arms wrapped around my face to protect it — tucking up my legs to make myself smaller, less of a target.

Wash up against a bunch of roots — grab hold — slippery — the wet roots feel like dead fingers clutching at me — a space between the water and the roof of the tunnel — I draw quick gasps of breath — current takes hold again — try fighting it — roots break off in my hands — swept away.

Tumbling over and over — hit my head hard on a rock — see stars — almost black out — struggle to keep head up — spit water out of my mouth, but more gushes in — feels like I'm swallowing half the stream.

The current drags me against a wall — sharp rocks cut deeply into my thighs and hips — freezing, cold water numbs the pain — stops the flow of blood — a sudden drop — plummet into a deep pool — down, down, down — held under by force of the falling water — panicking — can't find my way up — drowning — if I don't break free soon, I'll . . .

My feet strike a wall and propel me forward — drift slowly up and away from the pool — flow is gentle here — lots of space between water and top of tunnel — able to float along and breathe — air's cold, and it stings my lungs, but I gulp it down thankfully.

The stream opens out into what sounds like a large cave. Roars from the opposite end: the water must drop sharply again there. I let myself drift to one side before facing the drop. I need to rest and fill my lungs with air. As I tread water near the wall in the dark, something clutches at my bald head. It feels like twigs. I grab at them to steady myself, then realize they're not twigs — they're bones!

Too exhausted to be scared, I grasp the bones as though they were part of a life buoy. Taking long, deep breaths, I explore the bones with my fingers. They connect to a wrist, an arm, a body and head: a full skeleton. This stream was used to dispose of dead vampires in the past. This one must have washed up here and rotted away over the decades. I search blindly for other skeletons but find none. I wonder who the vampire was, when he lived, how long he's been here. It must be horrible, trapped in a cave like this, no proper burial, no final resting place.

I give the skeleton a shake, hoping to free it. The cave erupts with high-pitched screeches and flapping sounds. Wings! Dozens or hundreds of pairs of wings! Something crashes into my face and catches on my left ear. It scratches and bites. I yelp, tear it loose, and slap it away.

I can't see anything, but I sense a flurry of objects flying over and around me. Another collides with me. This time I hold on and feel it — a bat! The cave's full of bats. They must nest here, in the roof. The sound of me shaking the skeleton disturbed them, and they've taken flight.

I don't panic. They won't attack me. They're just frightened and will settle down soon. I release the one I've caught and let it join the rush above me. The noise dies down after a few minutes and the bats return to their perches. Silence.

I wonder how they get in and out of the cave. There must be a crack in the roof. For a few seconds I dream about finding it and climbing to safety, but my numb fingers and toes quickly put an end to these thoughts. I couldn't climb, even if I could find the crack and it was big enough for me to fit through.

I start thinking about the skeleton again. I don't want to leave it here. I tug at it, careful this time not to create a racket. It doesn't budge at first — it's wedged firm. I get a stronger grip and pull again. It comes loose, all at once, and falls on top of me, driving me under. Water gushes down my throat. Now I panic! The skeleton is heavy on top of me, weighing me down. I'm going to drown! I'm going to drown! I'm going to —

No! Stop panicking. Use my brain. I wrap my arms around the skeleton and slowly roll over. It works! Now the skeleton's underneath and I'm on top. The air tastes good. My heart stops pounding. A few of the bats are circling again, but most are still.

Releasing the skeleton, I guide it out towards the middle of the cave, using my feet. I feel the current take it, then it's gone. I hang on to the wall, treading water, giving the skeleton time to wash ahead of me. I start thinking while I wait: was it a good idea to free the skeleton? A nice gesture, but if the bones snag on a rock further along and block my way . . .

Too late to worry now. Should have thought of that before.

My situation is as desperate as ever. Crazy to think

I might get out of this alive. But I force myself to think positively: I've made it this far, and the stream must open up sooner or later. Who's to say I can't make it to the end? Believe, Darren, believe.

I'd like to hang here forever — easier to cling on and die of the cold — but I have to try for freedom. In the end, I force my fingers to unclench and let go of the bank. I drift out into the middle of the stream. The current bites at me and latches on. Speeding up — the exit — roaring grows furiously — flowing fast — angling sharply downwards — gone.

Grubbs Grady is about to learn three things:
The world is vicious. Magic is possible.
Demons are real.

Turn the page for a sneak peek at Darren Shan's
bloodcurdling new novel:

LORD LOSS

Book 1 in the DEMONATA series

Available now.

✤ Purgatory. Confined to my room after school for a month. A whole bloody *MONTH*! No TV, no computer, no comics, no books — except schoolbooks. Dad leaves my chess set in the room too — no fear my chess-crazy parents would take *that* away from me! Chess is almost a religion in this house. My sister Gret and I were reared on it. While other toddlers were being taught how to put jigsaws together, we were busy learning the ridiculous rules of chess.

I can come downstairs for meals, and bathroom visits are allowed, but otherwise I'm a prisoner. I can't even go out on the weekends.

In solitude, I call Gret every name under the moon the first night. Mom and Dad bear the brunt of my curses the next. After that I'm too miserable to blame anyone, so I sulk in moody silence and play chess against myself to pass the time.

They don't talk to me at meals. The three of them act like I'm not not there. Gret doesn't even glance at me spitefully and sneer, the way she usually does when I'm getting the doghouse treatment.

But what have I done that's so bad? OK, it was a crude joke and I knew I'd get into trouble — but their reactions are waaaaaaay over the top. If I'd done something to embarrass Gret in public, fair enough, I'd take what was coming. But this was a private joke, just between us. They shouldn't be making such a song and dance about it.

Dad's words echo back to me — "And the timing!" I think about them a lot. And Mom's, when she was going at me about smoking, just before Dad cut her short — "We don't need this, certainly not at this time, not when —"

What did they mean? What were they talking about? What does the timing have to do with anything?

Something stinks here — and it's not just rat guts.

✠ I spend a lot of time writing. Diary entries, stories, poems. I try drawing a comic — "Grubbs Grady, Superhero!" — but I'm no good at art. I get great marks in my other subjects — way better than goat-faced Gret ever gets, as I often remind her — but I've got all the artistic talent of a duck.

I play lots of games of chess. Mom and Dad are chess fanatics. There's a board in every room and they play several games most nights, against each other or friends from their chess clubs. They make Gret and me play too. My earliest memory is of sucking on a white rook while Dad explained how a knight moves.

I can beat just about anyone my age — I've won regional competitions — but I'm not in the same class as Mom, Dad, or Gret. Gret's won at national level and can wipe the floor with me nine times out of ten. I've only ever beaten Mom twice in my life. Dad — never.

It's been the biggest argument starter all my life. Mom and Dad don't put pressure on me to do well in school or at other games, but they press me all the time at chess. They make me read chess books and watch videotaped tournaments. We have long debates over meals and in Dad's study about legendary games and grandmasters, and how I can improve. They send me to tutors and keep entering me in competitions. I've argued with them about it — I'd rather spend my time watching and playing basketball — but they've always stood firm.

White rook takes black pawn, threatens black queen. Black queen moves to safety. I chase her with my bishop. Black queen moves again — still in danger. This is childish stuff — I could have cut off the threat five moves back, when it became apparent — but I don't care. In a petty way, this is me striking back. "You take my TV and computer away? Stick me up here on my own? OK — I'm gonna learn to play the worst game of chess in the world. See how you like that, Corporal Dad and Commandant Mom!"

Not exactly Luke Skywalker striking back against the evil Empire by blowing up the *Death Star*, I know, but hey, we've all gotta start somewhere!

✴ ✴ ✴

✚ Studying my hair in the mirror. Stiff, tight, ginger. Dad used to be ginger when he was younger, before the grey set in. Says he was fifteen or sixteen when he noticed the change. So, if I follow in his footprints, I've only got a handful or so years of unbroken ginger to look forward to.

I like the idea of a few grey hairs, not a whole head of them like Dad, just a few. And spread out — I don't want a skunk patch. I'm big for my age — taller than most of my friends — and burly. I don't look old, but if I had a few grey hairs, I might be able to pass for an adult in poor light — bluff my way into R-rated movies!

The door opens. Gret — smiling shyly. I'm nineteen days into my sentence. Full of hate for Gretelda Grotesque. She's the last person I want to see.

"Get out!"

"I came to make up," she says.

"Too late," I snarl nastily. "I've only got eleven

days to go. I'd rather see them out than kiss your . . ."

I stop. She's holding out a plastic bag. Something blue inside. "What's that?" I ask suspiciously.

"A present to make up for getting you grounded," she says, and lays it on my bed. She glances out of the window. The curtains are open. A three-quarters moon lights up the sill. There are some chess pieces on it, from when I was playing earlier. Gret shivers, then turns away.

"Mom and Dad said you can come out — the punishment's over. They've ended it early."

She leaves.

Bewildered, I tear open the plastic. Inside — a New York Knicks jersey, shorts and socks. I'm stunned. The Knicks are my team, my basketball champions. Mom used to buy me their latest gear at the start of every season, until I hit puberty and sprouted. She won't buy me any new gear until I stop growing — I outgrew the last one in just a month.

This must have cost Gret a fortune — it's brand new, not last season's. This is the first time she's ever given me a present, except at Christmas and birthdays. And Mom and Dad have never cut short a grounding before — they're very strict about making us stick to any punishment they set.

What the hell is going on?

✢ Three days after my early release. To say things are strange is the understatement of the decade. The atmosphere's just like it was when Grandma died. Mom and Dad wander around like robots, not saying much. Gret mopes in her room or in the kitchen, stuffing herself with sweets and playing chess non-stop. She's like an addict. It's bizarre.

I want to ask them about it, but how? "Mom, Dad — have aliens taken over your bodies? Is somebody dead and you're too afraid to tell me? Have you all converted to Miseryism?"

Seriously, jokes aside, I'm frightened. They're sharing a secret, something bad, and keeping me out of it. Why? Is it to do with me? Do they know something that I don't? Like maybe . . . maybe . . .

(Go on — have the guts! Say it!)

Like maybe *I'm* going to die?

Stupid? An overreaction? Reading too much into it? Perhaps. But they cut short my punishment. Gret gave me a present. They look like they're about to burst into tears at any given minute.

Grubbs Grady — on his way out? A deadly disease I caught on vacation? A brain defect that I've had since birth? The big, bad Cancer bug?

What other explanation is there?

✤ "Regale me with your thoughts on ballet."

I'm watching basketball highlights. Alone in the TV room with Dad. I cock my ear at the weird, out-of-nowhere question and shrug. "Rubbish," I snort.

"You don't think it's an incredibly beautiful art form? You've never wished to experience it first-hand? You don't want to glide across Swan Lake or get sweet with a Nutcracker?"

I choke on a laugh. "Is this a windup?"

Dad smiles. "Just wanted to check. I got a great offer on tickets to a performance tomorrow. I bought three — anticipating your less-than-enthusiastic reaction — but I could probably get an extra one if you want to tag along."

"No way!"

"Your loss." Dad clears his throat. "The ballet's out of town and finishes quite late. It will be easier for us to stay in a hotel overnight."

"Does that mean I'll have the house to myself?" I ask excitedly.

"No such luck," he chuckles. "I think you're old enough to guard the fort, but Sharon" — Mom — "has a different view, and she's the boss. You'll have to stay with Aunt Kate."

"Not no-date Kate," I groan. Aunt Kate's only a

couple of years older than Mom, but lives like a nine-ty-year-old. Has a black-and-white TV but only turns it on for the news. Listens to radio the rest of the time. "Couldn't I kill myself instead?" I quip.

"Don't make jokes like that!" Dad snaps with unex-pected venom. I stare at him, hurt, and he forces a thin smile. "Sorry. Hard day at the office. I'll arrange it with Kate, then."

He stumbles as he exits — as if he's nervous. For a minute there it was like normal, me and Dad mess-ing around, and I forgot all my recent worries. Now they come flooding back. If I'm not at death's door, why was he so upset at my throwaway gag?

Curious and afraid, I slink to the door and eaves-drop as he phones Aunt Kate and clears my stay with her. Nothing suspicious in their conversation. He doesn't talk about me as if these are my final days. Even hangs up with a cheery "Toodle-oo," a corny phrase he often uses on the phone. I'm about to with-draw and catch up with the basketball action when I hear Gret speaking softly from the stairs.

"He didn't want to come?"

"No," Dad whispers back.

"It's all set?"

"Yes. He'll stay with Kate. It'll just be the three of us."

"Couldn't we wait until next month?"

"Best to do it now — it's too dangerous to put off."

"I'm scared, Dad."

"I know, love. So am I."

Silence.

✣ Mom drops me off at Aunt Kate's. They exchange some small talk on the doorstep, but Mom's in a rush and cuts the conversation short. Says she has to hurry or they'll be late for the ballet. Aunt Kate buys that, but I've cracked their cover story. I don't know what Mom and Co. are up to tonight, but they're not going to watch a load of poseurs in tights jumping around like puppets.

"Be good for your aunt," Mom says, tweaking the hairs on my forehead.

"Enjoy the ballet," I reply, smiling hollowly.

Mom hugs me, then kisses me. I can't remember the last time she kissed me. There's something desperate about it.

"I love you, Grubitsch!" she croaks, almost sobbing.

If I hadn't already known something was very, very wrong, the dread in her voice would have tipped me off. Prepared for it, I'm able to grin and flip back at her, Humphrey Bogart style, "Love you too, shweet-heart."

Mom drives away. I think she's crying.

"Make yourself comfy in the living room," Aunt Kate simpers. "I'll fix a nice pot of tea for us. It's almost time for the news."

I make an excuse after the news. Sore stomach — need to rest. Aunt Kate makes me gulp down two large spoons of cod liver oil, then sends me up to bed.

I wait five minutes, until I hear Frank Sinatra crooning — no-date Kate loves Ol' Blue Eyes and always manages to find him on the radio. When I hear her singing along to some corny ballad, I slip downstairs and out the front door.

I don't know what's going on, but now that I know I'm not set to go toes-up, I'm determined to see it through with them. I don't care what sort of a mess they're in. I won't let Mom, Dad, and Gret freeze me out, no matter how bad it is. We're a family. We should face things together. That's what Mom and Dad always taught me.

Padding through the streets, covering the four miles home as quickly as I can. They could be any-where, but I'll start with the house. If I don't find them there, I'll look for clues to where they might be.

I think of Dad saying he's scared. Mom trembling as she kissed me. Gret's voice when she was on the stairs. My stomach tightens with fear. I ignore it, jog at a steady pace, and try spitting the taste of cod liver oil out of my mouth.

✤ Home. I spot a chink of light in Mom and Dad's bedroom, where the curtains just fail to meet. It doesn't mean they're in — Mom always leaves a light on to deter burglars. I slip around the back and peer through the garage window. The car's parked inside. So they're here. This is where it all kicks off. Whatever "it" is.

I creep up to the back door. Crouch, poke the dog flap open, listen for sounds. None. I was eight when our last dog died. Mom said she was never allowing another one inside the house — they always got killed on the roads and she was sick of burying them. Every few months, Dad says he must board over the dog flap or get a new door, but he never has. I think he's still secretly hoping she'll change her mind. Dad loves dogs.

When I was a baby, I could crawl through the flap. Mom had to keep me tied to the kitchen table to stop me from sneaking out of the house when she wasn't looking. Much too big for it now, so I fish under the pyramid-shaped stone to the left of the door and locate the spare key.

The kitchen's cold. It shouldn't be — the sun's been shining all day and it's a nice warm night — but it's like standing in a refrigerator aisle in a supermarket.

I creep to the hall door and stop, again listening for sounds. None.

Leaving the kitchen, I check the TV room, Mom's fancily decorated living room — off-limits to Gret and me except on special occasions — and Dad's study. Empty. All as cold as the kitchen.

Coming out of the study, I notice something strange and do a double-take. There's a chess board in one corner. Dad's prize chess set. The pieces are based on characters from the King Arthur legends. Hand-carved by some famous craftsman in the nineteenth century. Cost a fortune. Dad never told Mom the exact price — never dared.

I walk to the board. Carved out of marble, four inches thick. I played a game with Dad on its smooth surface just a few weeks ago. Now it's rent with deep, ugly gouges. Almost like fingernail scratches — except no human could drag their nails through solid marble. And all the carefully crafted pieces are missing. The board's bare.

Up the stairs. Sweating nervously. Fingers clenched tight. My breath comes out as mist before my eyes. Part of me wants to turn tail and run. I shouldn't be here. I don't *need* to be here. Nobody would know if I backed up and . . .

I flash back to Gret's face after the rat guts prank. Her tears. Her pain. Her smile when she gave me the Knicks jersey. We fight all the time, but I love her deep down. And not that deep either.

I'm not going to leave her alone with Mom and Dad to face whatever trouble they're in. Like I told myself earlier — we're a family. Dad's always said families should pull together and fight as a team. I want to be part of this — even though I don't know what "this" is, even though Mom and Dad did all they could to keep me out of "this," even though "this" terrifies me senseless.

The landing. Not as cold as downstairs. I try my bedroom, then Gret's. Empty. Very warm. The chess pieces on Gret's board are also missing. Mine haven't been taken, but they lie scattered on the floor and my board has been smashed to splinters.

I edge closer to Mom and Dad's room. I've known all along that this is where they must be. Delaying the moment of truth. Gret likes to call me a coward when she wants to hurt me. Big as I am, I've always gone out of my way to avoid fights. I used to think (*fear*) she might be right. Each step I take towards my parents' bedroom proves to my surprise that she was wrong.

The door feels red hot, as though a fire is burning behind it. I press an ear to the wood — if I hear the crackle of flames, I'll race straight to the phone and dial 911. But there's no crackle. No smoke. Just deep, heavy breathing . . . and a curious dripping sound.

My hand's on the doorknob. My fingers won't move. I keep my ear pressed to the wood, waiting . . . praying. A tear trickles from my left eye. It dries on my cheek from the heat.

Inside the room, somebody giggles — low, throaty, sadistic. Not Mom, Dad, or Gret. There's a ripping sound, followed by snaps and crunches.

My hand turns.

The door opens.

Hell is revealed.

What evil does Grubbs find behind the door?

Read all of **LORD LOSS**, Book 1 in the DEMONATA series, available now.

The Demonata exist in a multi-world universe of their own.
Evil, murderous creatures who revel in torment and slaughter.
They try to cross over into our world all the time.

Don't miss Darren Shan's
chilling DEMONATA series.

And watch out for *Bec* (Book 4),
coming May 2007.

Read all the books in Darren Shan's *New York Times*
bestselling CIRQUE DU FREAK series:

	DATE DUE	
APR 0 2 2007		
OCT 1 1 2007		
FEB 1 4 2008		
APR 3 0 2008		
sep 14		
SEP 1 7 2012		